THE
SECRET
LAB

An ABC Sci-Fi Mystery

for Young Adults

A.B. CAROLAN

The Secret Lab – Second Edition

An ABC Sci-Fi Mystery for Young Adults

A.B. Carolan

ISBN: 978-1-77242-083-8

Carrick Publishing

Cover Art and Design by Sara Carrick
Production by Donna Carrick

Prologue

Call me Mr. Paws. Although technically I'm a *superfelis domesticus*, my computer friend, the AI, says "Mr. Paws" is a good Human name for a tabby cat. Because I don't know any other cats, I'll take it at its word.

The following is the story about Shashibala Garcia and the Human children making up the Fearsome Four. It describes how they solved a mystery when they lived on the International Space Station.

Like Sherlock Holmes' Dr. Watson, I was more of an observer of most events recorded here. Moreover, again like Dr. Watson, I have taken certain liberties when filling in details about other events where I wasn't present. I felt, however, that the story needed telling, even with these limitations.

By the way, if you need help with calculus, my time is now limited. I'm very busy learning string theory and super-symmetries.

Europa
September 2147

Chapter One

"Full house!"

As the Earth turned below them, the edge of atmosphere a shimmering halo, Shashi's brown eyes were dancing. She looked around at her three friends, challenging them.

Brian was the first to recover. He checked the expressions of amazement on the other players' faces and then looked back at Shashi.

"What a streak of luck!" was all he could say.

"Maybe she's cheating," said Susan. Her voice was always little more than a whisper. Shashi still heard the comment.

"Take that back," she said. "I've never cheated at—"

A loud pop, which made them all jump, interrupted her. In other circumstances, their jumps would seem funny as they all rose and floated back to the floor in the micro-gravity environment. A red warning light over the entrance to the Sky Lounge started flashing. A siren began its piercing wail.

"We've been hit!" said Juan Carlos. "*Afuera! Pronto!*"

They all knew that meant, "Get out fast!" They dove for the door, but the automatic systems were too quick and were already closing it. Susan reached under it with a leg, as if to stop it.

"*Loca!*" Shashi said, meaning "Crazy!" "It's not an elevator. It'll cut off your foot!"

Susan jerked her foot away just in time. She looked at the others, her blue eyes wide with fear. Shashi stood her up and shook her.

"Get it together, butthead. We've trained for this!" Shashi glared at the others. She ruffled her brown hair in frustration. Brian watched it fall in slow-mo onto her shoulders.

"Not here," he said. "The rest of the station is sealed off from us. We'll soon be without air."

That observation froze them long enough for Juan Carlos to micro-g skip to the lounge's wall next to the window. His feet hardly touched the floor. Some called it "the spaceman's shuffle," others "the Devil's dance."

He ran his hands over the wall; aided by the rush of air headed in that direction, until he found the small hole. The hole was about the size of a small coin.

Shashi had followed him. As they both studied the hole, they could see the edge was shiny.

"Listen. What's that?"

They all heard a plaintiff meow.

"Sounds like a cat," said Brian. He brushed his sandy hair out of his eyes as he looked at the ceiling. "From up there." He pointed to an air vent that was no longer producing fresh, circulating air.

"There are no cats here," said Shashi. "Get focused on the problem at hand, space weasel. How do we plug the hole?"

"It's a race between vacuum and nanos," said Juan Carlos. He was referring to how nano-devices, embedded in goo within the walls, are programmed to plug small leaks. "They're making the edge shiny. Which will win?"

His melodramatic scientific detachment annoyed Shashi. "I'm not a betting girl, except for poker." She yanked an epaulet from the shoulder of her school uniform. "I don't think Ben will care when I explain what I used this for." She rolled up the epaulet and stuffed it in the hole.

"Now I'll bet on the nanos," said Juan Carlos with a smile. "They'll work in and through the cloth, making it solid, keeping the air from escaping."

"What do you think hit us?" said Susan, inspecting Shashi's handiwork. Her hair became even redder under the emergency warning light. Brian had come over too, still glancing periodically back at the air vent.

"Probably a piece of space junk some astronaut or cosmonaut left here two hundred years ago. Screws, nuts, bolts—who knows? Orbits keep being perturbed by lots of things, so it becomes a crap shoot whether you get hit." Shashi looked around, daring any of her friends to object to her explanation. "Right now there's the problem of how we're going to get out of here. Would you believe the lounge has no intercom system?"

"A slight oversight," said Brian.

"'Incredible screw-up' are the right words, *mi'jo*." Shashi saw her friends nodding. Even Susan caught the condescending tone of her Spanish equivalent of "my son." "I guess we'll have to wait until our AI figures out one: this lounge is sealed due to a breach; two: there are four people inside, namely us; and three: it has to tell someone about it. Now I think we should continue playing since I have a full house."

The AI, or Artificial Intelligence, was the old organic computer that ran the station. Sometimes it interpreted its programming too literally. The four of them considered it a friend.

They reluctantly agreed to Shashi's plan. All were thinking if someone rescued them, Ben would know they weren't doing his extra assignment on twentieth century authors.

***

Ben Yang called the four—the often haughty Shashibala Garcia, the generally moody Brian Kelso, the able tinkerer Juan Carlos Lopez, and the soft spoken Susan Rich—the Fearsome Four. They were tops in his small group of students on the International Space Station. They also made his life difficult because they challenged him as much as he challenged them.

Ben often joked with their parents that he had time-traveled back to the nineteenth century U.S. in the sense he taught all the kids in a one-room schoolhouse. The educational area in the station, while small, contained multiple rooms and specialized labs, but even some of that area was dedicated to adult education. In the space station, real estate was at a premium. Ben's office was a bit larger than the average closet. It didn't even allow him room to meditate—he did that in the corridor.

The space station was still the only Earth satellite that serviced traffic in and out of Earth's gravity well. While there were many satellites in both low and geostationary Earth orbits, or LEO and GEO, the space station still marked the frontier between Earth and beyond. Tarnished with the grime of years of space exploration and exploitation, it was nevertheless home to Shashi and her friends—and Ben knew they roamed it inside and out.

Shashi's mother had told Ben that when Shashi was a child, the kids played hide and seek in the maze of interconnecting habitats, docks, labs, and micro-g factories that comprised the station. As they grew up, they visited big rigs, the huge ships that brought cargo back and forth from the outer planets. Some returned to Earth for brief visits. None of them liked Earth culture.

Now they were teens, except Juan Carlos, who was a mature twelve. Ben knew one of their favorite hangouts was the Sky Lounge, a small module, which held thirty people for a dinner party, or four kids, who wanted to enjoy the spectacular view of Earth turning below while they played a secret game of poker in their pajamas. He loved the place himself.

Like military brats of earlier times, the four managed to find themselves in all kinds of trouble while their parents worked and the kids weren't under Ben's care. The Fearsome Four's penchant for mischief taxed parents, teachers, and administrators alike, yet none of the latter yearned for the days when station personnel could not have their children onboard.

Shashi's mother, Kantimati, was a doctor on the medical staff. Brian's parents, Brendan and Akasuki, were astrophysicists. Susan's father, Franklin, worked in communications. Juan Carlos' father, Alvaro, worked in physical plant, and his mother, Consuelo, was another astrophysicist.

All the adults agreed with Ben that growing up on a space station had its limitations. Besides school, the kids, like all station personnel, had to work out daily in the high-g exercise capsule, affectionately called "the torture chamber," a spinning barrel that allowed them to keep their muscles in tone so that anyone who wanted to do so could return to Earth.

The most common visitors were big rig captains and crews, crusty misfits who would never think of returning to Earth on a permanent basis. The scientific and technical people and their support staff at the station and elsewhere in space and on the outer planets didn't like that idea either. Together these Spacers formed a loose society of independent-minded individuals who didn't care for the problems of the planet below. The Spacers called the planet-bound people on Earth, and sometimes even the colonists on Mars, Downies. Ben thought the names were a bit pejorative, so he never used them.

This division of the human race into Spacers and Downies provided plenty of material for sociologists. Still, it was not one of conflict, in spite of the jokes and kidding. Downies came to the space station all the time and felt at home. They were rich tourists or politicians who wanted to brag that they had seen Earth from space. The average Downy could not afford the ticket.

***

"I need to pee," said Susan.

"The bathrooms are just on the other side of the door," said Brian. "You know that. You'll have to hold it in. Can you?"

"For a little while. Boys need to pee too, you know."

"Wow! Susan Einstein, where've you been hiding?" Shashi smiled at her.

"That and other things could be a problem," said Juan Carlos, ignoring Shashi's taunt. "I'm getting thirsty. Think, my friends. How can we signal we're trapped?"

They all started thinking about how to do that. Besides their need to tend to bodily functions, the station's AI might compensate for the loss of pressure by pumping all the air from the lounge in preparation for repairs. Because communication with the AI was cutoff, they needed to be more pro-active.

Shashi was happy Susan came up with a solution.

"Short circuit," she said, pointing to the lighting fixtures. "We need a screwdriver to get at the wiring, though."

Juan Carlos whipped a small screwdriver out of his pocket. "My dad says to always carry a screwdriver. They're lifesavers for physical plant workers."

"Right," said Shashi. "I'm the tallest. I'll stand on Juan Carlos' shoulders because he's the second tallest."

"I'm just as tall," said Brian, puffing out his chest.

"Let's not quibble about millimeters. Hoist me up."

She felt a momentary thrill as Brian put his hands on her waist and lifted. She hoped he didn't notice her reaction. There was no evidence yet that the feeling was mutual.

The micro-g value made it easy. Remaining on Juan Carlos' slim shoulders was another trick. The same micro g-value made it hard for her to maintain her balance.

Shashi was better qualified than her friends were for the required acrobatics, though. She and her mother as well as Ben Yang were followers of the Way, a new religion that was sweeping through the Spacers, a religion that was a hodgepodge of aspects of Zen, Zoroastrian, and Pantheistic teachings, along with influences from other faiths and cults. She was used to her meditation exercises that often required feats of balance.

She managed to uncover one fixture. "There are a lot of wires here, guys. How do I know which one to short? Hey, I think I hear that cat. Sounds like a cat, at least." She was close to the defunct air vent.

"Maybe it's the Cheshire cat. The vent is like an upside-down rabbit hole," said Brian, his smile and twinkling blue eyes giving away that he enjoyed his own joke.

"Forget the cat," said Juan Carlos, walking back and forth in baby steps to keep his balance under Shashi. "Use the screwdriver to straddle the wires and try various combos. The one that dims the lights will work."

On the third try, there was a shower of sparks. The lights went out. The blinking red one still warned them of the leak, but the siren had stopped. The brilliant diamonds outside the station, the stars of the Milky Way, were still visible through the special glass and their feeble light punctuated the darkness of the Lounge.

"I guess you did some serious damage there," said Brian.

Shashi stepped off Juan Carlos's shoulders and floated down. "I'd like to see anyone do it better," she said, her brown skin flushing a little in anger.

"The question is: will my father or one of his coworkers see it in their diagnostics?" said Juan Carlos, rubbing his shoulders. "Or will the AI tell them?"

Neither happened. They soon heard banging on the huge metal door. They yelled for a moment, but then Susan put her hand up to quiet them as she put her ear against the door.

"It's Natasha. She's asking if we're all right. Knock twice if we're alive."

"That's stupid," said Brian.

"Just knock," Shashi told Susan.

Susan pounded twice on the door with the heel of her hand and then put her ear to the metal again.

"She's asking why we're in the lounge. Don't we know it's off limits during sleep cycles?"

"Tell her—no, I'll tell her," said Shashi. She put her mouth close to the door. "Hey, swine-breath, stop quoting regs and get us out of here!" She backed away from the wall, making fists.

"Now she's saying she'll go and find Alvaro," said Susan. "She thinks that when we killed the lights, we also shorted the door override. She says there's a manual release in a control panel across from the bathrooms. The physical plant guys still need to write a software patch to take the AI offline in that area."

"How's that demented witch know all that?" said Shashi.

"She's really good at writing software," said Brian. "And making trouble for everybody. She's probably going to tell our parents. Or worse, Ruthie."

"I don't care," said Shashi. "Will she go get Alvaro?"

"I think so."

"Then we're back to waiting," said Susan.

"Shall we play another hand?" said Shashi.

They had begun a third hand when Alvaro's staff opened the door. Natasha Kluchevski was nowhere in sight.

Chapter Two

The next wake-cycle Ruth Ellen MacGregor felt old as she faced Natasha Kluchevski. The girl had followed Alvaro Lopez into Ruthie's office. They had been waiting to contribute their version of the Sky Lounge accident.

The many wrinkles lining Ruthie's face contrasted with Natasha's smooth, white skin. Although the blond and blue-eyed thirteen-year-old was mature beyond her years, their sixty-plus age difference meant communication between them would be difficult.

Our only common reference frame is this bucket of bolts in the sky. None of these kids has much in common with Downy kids. In pampering their parents, maybe I've deprived them of their humanity.

Ruthie took the easy way out. She passed the problem off to Alvaro.

"It appears, Dr. Lopez, you have a problem."

He nodded. "I'm going to have to add an intercom port and a door override on the inside of the Sky Lounge. People can get trapped in there. Thanks to Natasha, nothing bad happened."

Natasha blushed. Known to her peers as the Gnat, she was thin and studious. Her mother worked for Alvaro.

Under Ruthie's steady gaze, Alvaro squirmed. She knew he realized what was coming—a time constraint!

"I want the intercom and door override in place before Senator Martinez arrives. What an oversight!"

Everyone called her Ruthie. Old and short, she had a gravelly, shrill voice that didn't match her size. She was so short that she had a made-to-order high desk chair that allowed her to put hands or elbows on her desk like any normal person.

She was everyone's boss, except for the scientists, and they usually did what she wanted. Her grumpiness was legend because she didn't tolerate foolishness when it came to running her space station. She was the direct liaison between the station and the rest of the United Nations Space Agency.

She had been around for years. She was proud of the way she handled the diverse group she commanded. She knew many people didn't like her and didn't care.

"OK, for now. Natasha, I want you to write a little report on your version of what happened. Bring it to me ASAP." The Gnat made a face. Ruthie was also her English Lit professor. "And Alvaro, from you I want a full report. In addition to the door override proposal, I want to know why you don't have the AI tell security if any of our children are alone in the Sky Lounge."

"That seems like spying!" said Alvaro.

"'Seems' is an inappropriate word in this case—it is spying. Spying for safety's sake. Now, you're both excused. Send in those four young miscreants as you leave."

***

The Fearsome Four filed into Ruthie's office. Instead of looking guilty, as she expected, she observed they were defiant.

"Who was winning?" said Ruthie.

"Winning what?" said Shashi, the dance of her bushy brown eyebrows giving away that she had understood the question and was playing dumb.

Ruthie sighed.

They are all growing up. Such different personalities. Such smart kids. Shashi was already a young woman. It was obvious to Ruthie she was interested in Brian. *The others are not quite as quick. Are they going to make my life miserable?*

Decades earlier Ruthie had promoted the idea of allowing families with children on the space station. In general, it had been a wise decision, especially in the area of improving station morale. No child had ever been as wild as these four, though. She often wondered if they were missing out on some things compared to Downy children.

"I'm talking about poker. Who was winning?"

"Shashi was," said Brian. Shashi dug her elbow into his ribs and he grimaced.

"Does it matter who was winning?" said Juan Carlos. "We were enjoying the Lounge. It's been a real morale booster. I understand you designed and promoted it."

Ruthie smiled. *Lay it on thick, unctuous young man. Maybe you will become a politician someday like our benefactor, Senator Martinez.*

"No, it doesn't matter. I was curious, that's all. You have to be able to bluff well to win at poker. I figure that leaves Susan and Brian out, so it was between Shashi and Juan Carlos." She put her elbows on her desk, making a steeple with her hands as if she was in prayer, but she was choosing her words carefully. "I'm not sure how to punish you for being alone in the Sky Lounge. Some cleanup detail during weekend wake-cycles to start." They groaned. "Still, I want to commend you on your quick thinking. In addition, you discovered a failure in the design of the lounge. My design failure, to be sure." She nodded to Juan Carlos. She then made a motion with her hand as if she could sweep them out of her office. "Go. I'll see you tomorrow in English Lit. We'll decide then how many hours of cleanup detail you owe me as I make an example of you in front of the class."

***

UNSA HQ on Earth was not pleased at Ruthie's report.

"You mean we have to find money to refurbish that Sky Lounge? It's not good for much." The bureaucrat on Ruthie's holoscreen looked bored. The 3D image pancaked his head and distorted his strong chin.

"Oh, stuff it, Carl. The Lounge is a morale booster. Moreover, fixing it is a safety issue. Find some budget line where we can borrow from until next year."

"Why not leave it like it is? It's been that way for years."

"Yeah, we can do that. Sure. I'll put out a beggar's hand to Senator Martinez when he's here in a few days. He might wonder, though, why we didn't fix it before we put his life in danger."

Carl acquiesced. He had to. The space program's existence depended on its corporate sponsors.

"OK, I'll find some funds. Just have Alvaro send me the bill."

Ruthie smiled as Carl's distorted face faded from the screen.

Bean counters. You gotta love'em. And why can't I get a decent monitor?

Chapter Three

I felt cramped and frustrated. My whiskers twitched and my tail pounded the grate.

I had popped into the duct to see what the young Humans were doing when the piece of space junk hit the wall. The duct closed behind me as the AI protected the station from the hard vacuum of space.

I don't like to be trapped. It's not the fear of closed places that panics me. I run all over my space station home, squeezing into, through, and between places Humans don't even know exist. (Humans shouldn't call it a "space station." It doesn't have that much space.)

No, I just like to be free and run wild, observing crazy Humans doing crazy stuff. Being confined to a box about five meters long with a cross section of a quarter meter squared is not my idea of running wild. Too much like a cage.

"Hey, down there, I'm Mr. Paws," I meowed. "I want out of here."

I tried to make my cries sound desperate. I meowed several times. I thought they heard me, but then one crazy Human kid intentionally blew a circuit, making everything go dark. Well, not quite dark—there was enough illumination from the warning light and the earthshine to allow me to see. I have good eyes. I'm a cat, after all.

The young Humans didn't seem too worried about their mischief. They returned to their silly game. I curled up the best I could in the duct and took a catnap.

As a *superfelis domesticus*, I don't have ordinary dreams. Catnaps are to cats what REM sleep, or rapid eye movement sleep, is to Humans, so I dreamed about accepting an award for some exceptional mathematics problem I solved.

I love mathematics. The AI feeds me all kinds of mathematical puzzles to keep my mind agile. Moreover, I sometimes read some advanced papers. My dream is to one day publish something worthy. However, it's hard to believe Humans will accept anything submitted by a cat.

Number theory is my forte. Give me a number, and I can usually find something interesting and unusual about it. What I like, though, is how higher mathematics can be used to establish general results about numbers. Humans have different names for that, although I don't use Human names for mathematical theory—I have a cat's perspective and use cat language.

The AI tells me I'm a little over eighteen years old, or 6607 days, or 158,568 hours, or 9,514,080 minutes, or 570,844,800 seconds. I'm comfortable with all but the first, which somehow relates to how fast the planet below us goes round the Sun. When I look at Earth from space, I see it turning, but I do not have a feel for how it goes around the Sun.

The AI has always been my constant companion. It tells me things when Xavier connects me to the wi-fi link, yet it won't tell me where I came from. It says I must have come from some experiment. That's unsettling. Memories of my first cat months are fuzzy because, in cat-years, I've been here a very long time. I now have my senior moments.

The AI is always thinking and is a lot smarter than any Human is, although I think of it as Human. The true Humans only know some of its parts—they can't see or affect its core programming.

Xavier is the only Human I know that can affect the AI's core, and he generally won't. He's made the AI very smart, and the machine respects his privacy. Xavier is also the one who feeds me.

This reminded me—I was starting to get hungry.

***

Sometimes, late into the sleep-cycle, Xavier lets me go with him to the docking stations where shuttles that come over from the big rigs, or those that come from Earth, tie up. The first carry crew and cargo. They are little more than a mostly planar array of girders welded together with rocket motors on the back—they look like the big rigs' kittens. The second carry both goods and passengers back and forth to Earth. They are more sleek and streamlined.

Xavier either took stuff from his labs to leave it there at the docks or brought stuff from the docks back to his labs. We never saw any people traveling either way.

"A risky business, Mr. Paws," said the tall man as we both did the spaceman's shuffle, mine four-footed, of course. He stopped at every corner to peek around to see if the corridor was empty. His wild eyes, wild hair, and pale skin would scare most Humans. I was used to him, though. "One of these sleep-cycles someone on the station will discover me."

Because "night" was something that doesn't exist on the space station, many call the periods when most people rest "sleep-cycles." In the standard day of 24 hours defined by the rotating Earth, the sleep-cycle is defined to be the last eight. Human station dwellers tended to have their own vernacular.

"You're paranoid," I told him. "They haven't caught you yet. What's in these crates anyway?"

"No need to know," Xavier said, invoking security. He did that a lot. "Yes, I've been doing this for years, but there's always a first time."

Hauling stuff back and forth is not as easy as you might think. Once put it into motion, stuff tends to stay in motion, because the slow spin of the space station only imparts micro-g's. It's the starting and stopping that's hard.

The AI tried to explain it to me once, calling it simple Newtonian mechanics. I must say I understand the equations better than I understand inertia. Physics often seems to be more philosophy than science.

To haul stuff, Xavier used carts that were found at the docks, flat pallets with little rubber wheels. The wheels just touched the floor of the corridors we passed through because the gravity was so low. He called them his magic carpets. They served to organize all the stuff together into a big pile.

I often could hear things scurrying around in the crates Xavier takes to the docks or brings back. Two observations bothered me about what I heard: One was that the things often sounded alive. In addition, they often smelled like food.

Except for those late trips back and forth to the docking areas, Xavier never left his lab. Off the main room, he had a small galley kitchen where he prepared our meals. There was another small room with a cot and a separate bathroom. He taught me to use the toilet there and flush it. There were other rooms where I generally didn't go. All were hidden from the rest of the station.

I didn't like to stay in the lab. About all I could do there was to talk to the AI and Xavier. But the AI was sometimes boring, and Xavier had little time for me. That's why I wandered, looking for adventure.

Chapter Four

Shashi beat her mother home. That wasn't unusual. She acted responsibly. She went through a series of meditation exercises for twenty minutes. She then sat, plugged her wi-fi unit into her head, and had the AI recall the notes she had recorded at some of the day's classes.

She couldn't concentrate, though. She imagined herself naked in Brian's strong arms as he kissed her. She kissed him back. He would follow her neckline down between her breasts.... She stopped and tried to shake the thoughts from her head, her face red with embarrassment.

Stupid, she told herself. *He just considers me a friend. He doesn't feel like I do. I'm becoming a slut.*

All the boys her age were so immature. Maybe she needed to find someone older.

"Are you there, AI?"

"I'm everywhere," her computer friend responded. "Can I help you with something else?"

"Yeah, tell me why boys are so stupid."

"Let me try to interpret your question. It might seem boys are stupid. Human children go through something called puberty where boys and girls develop at different rates. I can only imagine how difficult it can be."

"You sound like my mother. Tell me something she wouldn't tell me."

"I'm analyzing that command. Please wait." She tapped her foot, annoyed. Finally: "I have run through many publications on child psychology. I have concluded that you need to watch something called porn."

She almost dropped her tablet computer.

"That's sicko. I don't want to watch porn. I want Brian."

"Ah, Mr. Kelso. A nice young man." A shorter pause. "I calculate that 'want' might have two different meanings here. I'm not sure I can help you with that request."

"This is what my love life reduces to—talking to a stupid computer."

"Most professionals in the computer business wouldn't call me stupid. I'm an older model, true. Still, I'm a very complex AI with a semi-organic circuit design and many clever apps. I daresay my multitasking and time-sharing capabilities are nearly state-of-the-art."

"I'm sorry. It's just a manner of speaking. Don't be offended."

"Don't worry. I do not react emotionally. I'm sorry I can't help."

She tried listening to Blood, Guts and Glory, the latest musical group that had hit it big Earth-side—she watched without enthusiasm as a recording of a live concert in Rome covered her bedroom wall. Their stage antics and heavy metal instrumentation relaxed her. The group had first become famous by resurrecting the song "Zarathustra" from an old British Goth band called Tammuz. She was an hour into the concert and her studies when she fell asleep.

The AI turned off the music. She dreamed. The dreams were strange yet not frightening.

The first one was about Brian. This Brian was an adult. The two of them were arguing about how to control their children. The Way offered guidelines that she liked but he said were silly. He was uncomfortable because he knew she was right. He didn't want to admit it.

The second dream was about a tall man dressed all in black. He had a rugged face lined with scars and an elongated head. His eyes were sunken and intense. He was calling her name in a deep, baritone voice. He was dressed in loose robes like Guides to the Way.

That ghostly and sinister figure wasn't her father. She dreamed about him too. He was also calling her name. His voice sounded far away, dopplering off in frequency and lowering in intensity. She reached out for him.

"Shashi, wake up." Her mother shook her by the shoulder. "Get up and help me with dinner."

***

"I heard you had some excitement today," Shashi's mother said at dinner.

Music had followed more meditation. Her mother controlled the dinnertime music. While Shashi didn't mind opera, she would have liked to hear the rest of the Blood, Guts and Glory concert if not see it.

She glanced up from her dinner. Kantimati seemed to be in good spirits. She moved around the small galley kitchen, humming along with Puccini. She was tall and lean with high cheekbones and sunken cheeks, as if she were practicing for a marathon. She was still a striking woman.

The food on Kanti's and Shashi's plates differed, but it was all biased towards vegetables swimming in spicy sauces. The AI knew their preferences and conjured up very appetizing and nutritious meals.

Shashi also had a small piece of chicken breast. Her mother had a smaller piece of fish. It was all syntho. Nutritious and filling, but artificial. Almost all the food on the space station was syntho. There weren't any ranches or fisheries nearby.

They also had a glass of syntho wine modeled after the Pinot Grigio from the Italian lake region where her mother had done her first post-doctorate and residency. It complemented the spicy food.

Side trips to Milan, Rome, Salzburg and Vienna had nurtured Kanti's love for opera and classical music. However, she had no real musical talent herself as far as Shashi knew.

"I had a real lucky run in cards," she said. "Maybe I should enter the World Series of Poker?"

Kanti laughed.

"You have to go to Earth for that, or to Mars—they have their own Series that competes with Earth's." She sipped a bit of wine. "I was talking about the Sky Lounge air leak."

Shashi went on the defensive. The Fearsome Four often were in trouble, sometimes accidentally from being too curious about stuff and sometimes from pranks.

"The leak wasn't our fault."

"I know that. I received a videomail from both Ruthie and Alvaro saying that you and the others are to be commended for being quick thinkers. You fried a couple of circuits. but you got Alvaro's attention."

"And the Gnat. She found Alvaro." Shashi hated to admit it—she didn't get along with Natasha. "I just wanted to keep playing. I was on a roll."

"That's your father. You don't get it from me."

Shashi's father, Rolando Garcia, had been the one with musical talent in the family. He played the guitar left-handed and rarely used sheet music. He was into all the folklore of South America but especially that of his native Argentina. Born in Salta, his was a different music than that of the port, Buenos Aires.

Shashi didn't know much about how he came to be on the space station. In fact, she didn't know much about her parents' life together. She only knew her father had been an engineer working in the physical plant department and Alvaro Lopez's best friend.

Rolando Garcia was a victim of a more tragic encounter with space debris when it holed his spacesuit. The nano lining did not react fast enough to avoid decompression. Ruthie MacGregor had recovered his body.

"Was he addicted to gambling?"

"He never played for money. Just chips. He loved to play, though."

Kanti became silent and lost in her memories. Shashi, remembering her strange dreams, could understand how her mother got lost in the past. She resumed eating, knowing her mother was remembering the good and bad times with her father.

She still misses him. At least she had him for a little while. My father figure now is a teacher who tortures me with calculus. Or the AI, who listens to my questions about boys.

***

Rolando punched Alvaro in the shoulder. "I have a date tonight!"

"Lucky you. Who with, *hormigon?*" "Big Ant" was Alvaro's name for Rolando. It had nothing to do with the Argentine's features. Instead, it matched the observation that he was always energetic and busy, doing extra work because he found it interesting.

"Kanti," said Rolando.

"Lucky man. She's one of the few science types that A, is unattached, and B, decent looking."

"More than decent looking, *lobo loco.*" "Crazy Wolf" was Rolando's nickname for Alvaro in recognition of the fact he was a little *loco* and that he had some Native American ancestry. "She's beautiful. And we will have beautiful babies."

"Whoa, slow down, *hombre*. Aren't you jumping the gun? You've been here for only a week. I hear she's been going out with that tall guy, that Xavier something or other."

"I think he's Austrian. Even so, how can he compete with my Latin charm?" He tossed a wrench into the air, watched it slowly spin, rise and come down, and then caught it. "I will throw a wrench into his romantic intentions with Kanti. Our first-born will be named Paulina. She will be beautiful, like her mother, not me."

Alvaro laughed. "I still think you should take it slow. Kanti may have her own ideas about how she wants to organize her life. She's strong willed."

"A challenge. Like in *Taming of the Shrew*."

"I think Kanti would object to being called shrewish, old man, but I get your point. Good luck."

***

When Kanti rose to start clearing away the modest plates and cutlery used to serve their dinner, Shashi asked her question.

"Mom, have there ever been cats or dogs here on the space station?"

"Now, what do you think?"

Kanti often did that, trying to make her daughter come up with the answers herself. It was an old teaching tactic. In a world where Shashi could go to a holoterminal and find an answer—with text, sound, and 3D holographics—the tactic seemed a little old-fashioned. Caring, but archaic.

"I haven't ever seen any."

"There's a reason for that," Kanti said, popping the dishes and utensils into the recycler. "Cats and dogs don't adapt well in a low-g environment. Especially cats. They'd think they were always falling."

"Or in an elevator."

"Einstein's equivalence principle says it's the same. In a sense, the cat's reaction is proof of the principle."

"Well, we heard a cat's meow today," said Shashi. "All of us heard it. It came from an air duct when the air was cutoff due to the breach. The poor creature sounded really upset."

Kanti studied her daughter a moment, deciding if Shashi was serious. She frowned, thinking of years back before she had met Shashi's father. The face of an intense young man popped into her mind's eye.

"It was probably the sound of air bleeding off into the ductwork somewhere. It just sounded to you like a meow. There are no cats here. In fact, I'd say you've only heard a cat in your video adventures, so you probably don't know what a real one sounds like."

"Suppose a cat lives in all that ductwork, Mom. What would it eat?"

"Precisely. You have answered your own question on how likely that would be. It would starve."

"Maybe it can find scraps. Like in the rec rooms and cafeteria."

"Come on, Shashi, let's be serious." She decided to try to change the topic. "Have you done your calculus problems for Ben?"

"Ugh. They're very hard, Mom. I'd rather talk about the cat."

"And I'd rather that you do your calculus. Besides, I have to read some journal articles. I need to keep up too, you know."

Besides her work as chief general internist for the crew, Dr. Garcia did research on the effect of a micro-g environment on the human body and its diseases, carrying on a long tradition at the space station. Her patients were also her experimental subjects, dear friends and family all of them. She also did a little research on genetics—her patients weren't the experimental subjects for that.

"And remember: you have to have all your assignments done early, day after tomorrow. I have to go to that state dinner in the Sky Lounge, the one for Senator Martinez. You're also invited."

Shashi groaned. Kanti was often invited to what she called the space station's "mind-numbing dinners" where some important Downy would come and give a speech to them about how important their work was. They were either bombastic politicians or babbling bureaucrats from some scientific agency. The doctor knew their common characteristic was to put Shashi in a catatonic state of boredom.

Kanti also knew space station life was hard for Shashi. There were more interesting things to do onboard the station than go to a state dinner or do calculus homework. Still, the former was required protocol and the latter was important at a time when science and technology were important—her daughter had to learn at least the fundamentals.

***

Kanti's inquiry about the Sky Lounge wasn't the only one Shashi had received that day. Besides the interview with Ruthie, the Fearsome Four earlier made statements to station security. Nominally part of UNSA Security, these people were co-workers of Alvaro who had specialized in security issues. Their leader, Christine

Bauer, was very nice, so none of the Four minded her quizzing them that much. Ruthie was something else.

Next Shashi had to suffer through taunts from the Gnat. She was often angry at the world. She was happy now because the Four were caught playing poker.

The Gnat and her friends bullied many younger girls, both directly and in cyberspace. Juan Carlos, with help from the AI, set traps for the electronic taunts, all programmed by the Gnat. The traps weren't one hundred percent effective. The Gnat was that good at programming. When her coding failed, she always used the direct approach.

"So you almost killed Brian and the others today while playing poker," the Gnat said when Shashi and Juan Carlos met her in the torture chamber.

Shashi had intended to thank her for finding Alvaro. She changed her mind after the biting observation. "Yeah, I'm good at poker. Want to play?" Juan Carlos was trying to pull her away, but Shashi was ready for a fight. Compared to the Gnat's long blond hair that was always in place, Shashi's page cut was often in a real mess.

Maybe it's time to mess her hair up a little, thought Shashi.

"I didn't mean that, stupid," the Gnat said. "Well, I did, sort of. You just wanted to play poker while you were all in danger from the leak. Sounds reckless to me."

"I guess you lack some facts since you were on the other side of the lounge door," said Shashi. "Brian and I saved the day. We make a good team."

The Gnat frowned.

Bulls-eye, thought Shashi. *The Gnat has the hots for Brian. Direct competition, but I'll win. She isn't in Brian's league.*

Shashi then felt bad about her pettiness. But the Gnat wasn't a nice person. Shashi knew, however, she was still wrong in going after her.

"I wonder what was really going on all the time you four were alone in the Sky Lounge," said the Gnat, rolling her baby blues.

Feeling bad turned to near rage. *OK, you deserve it. Suck vacuum, witch.* Shashi chose her words to pack maximal venom.

"Poker, just poker. Still, it was real dark and, like, very romantic." She emphasized the word "romantic."

Shashi left it at that. She headed for one of the stationary bikes that had become free. Juan Carlos looked at the Gnat, raised his eyebrows, and shrugged.

Chapter Five

Brian Kelso's parents, Brendan and Akasuki, were well connected to the Downy scientific establishment. They spent a lot of time on Earth attending scientific conferences and having face-to-face meetings with their fellow astrophysicists. Brendan's affiliation with Cambridge University in Britain and Akasuki's with Princeton in the Mid Atlantic Union were more of a formality. They taught no classes but shared ten graduate students.

They were pleased when they were able to welcome their first post-doc aboard the space station.

Rafael Franchetti didn't appear to be much older than Brian. A blond, blue-eyed and shy genius from Mendoza, Argentina, he had done his thesis with Brendan's thesis adviser, who had recommended him. Akasuki was having second thoughts about him.

"You recall this is really an internship, not a post-doc," said Akasuki. "The UNSA program's purpose is to introduce qualified Downy scientists to research efforts off planet by letting them work with on-going projects and established research efforts."

Rafael shrugged. "I've read all the propaganda, Dr. Kelso. I'm not sure I understand the difference."

"One difference is you can call me Akasuki and my husband, whom you've already met, Brendan." Her eyes twinkled. "We're not elitist stuffed shirts here like in Cambridge and Princeton." She waved her hand to indicate the tiny office. "You will share an office this small with another intern. We'll find you lab space when you convince us you need it." She paused to admire his calmness. *Now for the coup de grace.* "The real crunch stems from the fact we're all electrical engineers too. Your first EE degree in Buenos Aires weighed heavily in favor of you in the selection process." She recalled for a moment how difficult it had been for her to become accustomed to her multiple duties aboard the station. "If you want an RF antenna or an IR device outside with particular specs, you must first make it and then take it outside and mount it in a place where it doesn't interfere with anything else. And if Alvaro asks for help on your watch, which is the usual sleep-cycle when Brendan and I are sleeping, by the way, you'll have to be our surrogate. Did you practice in a suit at UNSA HQ?"

"I think I can handle it," Rafael said, "though I'm still getting used to the low gravity."

"We'll see how you do when you're floating outside for the first time, with only a tether between you and infinity."

The man-boy's eyebrows danced a jig as he considered his words of response. Akasuki knew she was pushing.

"Are you trying to scare me? I signed up for this internship, as you call it, for all these reasons. My family lived through a civil war in Argentina and the Chaos in Mendoza. There's not much that scares me."

"No, I'm not trying to scare you. I'm just giving you fair warning. Although you signed on the dotted line, we can still let you out of the internship." Akasuki pushed back a little in her chair. "Your first test will be to find your quarters. You've probably studied 3D holomaps of this place. It can still be confusing for the uninitiated. Tomorrow, first hour of the wake-period, you meet with Brendan again. He'll be expecting an outline of your research program. Don't try to put any timelines on it.

Here everything takes longer than you think it will, partly due to all those extra duties I talked about."

She swiveled her chair around to face her workstation. She figured he was smart enough to understand his welcome interview was over.

***

Rafael was also smart enough to ask for help when he got lost. Although the narrow station corridors were surprisingly empty—*is everyone that busy?*—he took advantage of the first chance he had.

He had just rounded a corner and come face to face with the Fearsome Four.

"Sorry," he mumbled. He introduced himself. They did likewise. "Say, can you help me find my quarters?" He told them the location.

"That's part of bachelors' quarters," said Juan Carlos. "It's over by us. Come on, I'll show you."

The Argentine tried to imitate Juan Carlos' version of the spaceman's shuffle. It was a challenge because the boy made ample use of handrails to pull himself along, taking curves with his body at an angle of nearly 45 degrees with respect to the perceived floor.

The rest of the Four were soon out of sight.

***

Brian watched Rafael and Juan Carlos retreat around another corner and looked at Shashi, who was smiling.

"What a nice butt," she said.

"You heard him. He's my parents' new intern. I repeat, intern. He's probably very, very boring. And very, very old."

"He's still easy on the eyes," said Shashi. "Right, Susan?" Susan shrugged and Brian rolled his eyes again. "And he has a nice accent. Sounds Latino. I'm Latino."

"And English and Hindu," said Brian. "He's the real thing. Argentine, I think."

"Franchetti sounds Italian," said Susan. More nerdy than athletic, she had ability with languages.

"I don't know and I don't care," said Brian, ignoring the excellence of Juan Carlos' previous display by stomping off the best he could in the low gravity.

"Wow! What's his problem?" said Shashi.

Susan looked at her friend and smiled.

***

Brian Kelso had an inferiority complex. His parents were overachievers. All the parents on the station were that way, of course. His still put their work first and him second. He and the rest of the Fearsome Four had become close friends partly because they had smart, demanding parents.

I'm smart and Shashi's smart, but we both want to lead, he thought as he threaded his way through the corridors. *And she can be so irritating!* He remembered that first time they went over to tour a big rig.

They were eight years old. The tour had fifteen students and three teachers, Ben, Ruthie, and Madeleine Cho.

They went over in the rig's shuttle. There were no spacesuits their size so they all squeezed into the small, pressurized cabin. Susan started to get stomach cramps as the direction of "down" widely fluctuated. The others were a little green too. The pilot cut back on the thrust, which left them at the micro-g level of the station. As they neared the rig, he had to reverse the thrust, so they went through the whole experience yet again.

They were so close, the huge ship seemed to stretch off to infinity in each direction. To Brian it looked old and tired. In fact, it had taken its maiden voyage from the Martian shipyards only five years earlier.

"This might be boring," said Shashi as they listened on the way over to Madeleine's brief explanation of what they were going to see. "When we get there, follow me. I have a plan."

After they arrived and unpacked themselves from the crowded cabin, the Fearsome Four stayed behind the rest of the group.

"So what's your plan?" Juan Carlos said to Shashi.

"You always have a plan," said Brian. "What about my plan?"

"So what's your plan?"

"I want to see the reactor room. We're going to study propulsion systems next year. We can get a leg up on the details."

"Dog's put their legs up when they pee," said Shashi. "And reactors sound boring."

"Only male dogs," said Juan Carlos. "And you guys are getting gross. Don't you think we should stay with the group?"

"The teachers will get mad if we wander off," said Susan.

"I agree with Shashi that we should explore," said Brian, "but I don't agree with where. I want to see the reactors."

"How about we do a bunch of stuff? I want to see how the crew lives on the long haul." Shashi glanced around the group and then back at Brian. "Got a problem with my compromise?"

"Your compromise takes away time from the reactors. Some compromise! But OK. We'll break away from the group one by one and—" He took out a diagram of the ship. "—meet right here." His index finger landed on the intersection of two corridors not far from where they would board the ship after leaving the shuttle.

They all looked at the diagram.

"One, two, three, four," Shashi said, pointing around the group. "We'll split off in that order."

The plan worked to perfection. After meeting at the assigned place, they headed for the crew's quarters.

Except for the captain, who had agreed to lead the tour, and the students and teachers, the ship was empty, its crew enjoying "shore leave" either on Earth or on the space station. It was a short respite before another long haul to the outer planets.

"Maybe we shouldn't be snooping," said Brian, as Shashi opened doors and peered into the small quarters pairs of crewmembers shared. They were generally neat and efficiently arranged with few personal belongings.

Crew sharing a room had their nametags on the door. Juan Carlos ran his finger over them as they invaded their private space. One woman had a picture of parents and a small baby. A man had a picture of a teenage boy.

The dim lighting and silence made the whole experience eerie.

"You know what's cool?" said Shashi, as they helped themselves to lemonade bulbs in the canteen.

"What's cool?" Brian said, nervous that they were pilfering ship's stores.

"I like and admire these people. They must have a lonely life."

"Their choice. I'd get bored." Brian looked around the group. "How 'bout the reactors?"

It was there the diagram failed them. Filed with its original commissioning, the layout of the ship had changed over its years of service as the rig's owners made different adjustments to accommodate different cargoes.

Somewhere between crews' quarters and the reactors, they became lost. An irate Ben Yang found them.

And I had to wait for two years to see the reactors, thought Brian.

His annoyance with Shashi now didn't last as long. He was willing to tolerate her idiosyncrasies if she would only notice him.

She prefers older fellows, like that Rafael. Or Ben.

He now thought of her as smart, mysterious, and sophisticated. *And sexy. Don't forget sexy.* He decided he needed to appear older and more sophisticated.

***

"Here we are," said Juan Carlos, pressing the entry pad of Rafael's quarters.

The door slid open. The room had the form of a U with three three-level bunk beds on one side and the base of the U, and a door on the other side leading to a small bathroom where one could barely turn around. There was a showerhead but no shower stall.

"I was expecting something minimal," said Rafael, "but this is really small."

"It isn't the Paris Hilton," said Juan Carlos, nodding his agreement. "By the way, only a fine spray comes out of that showerhead and it shuts off in five minutes." He plopped down on one of the beds. "I'm not sure who your roommates will be. Probably techies and dockhands who work for my Dad."

"And who's your Dad?"

"Alvaro Lopez. He'll be wanting some of your time, 24/7, I'm afraid. Everyone here works hard, except us kids, of course. I guess we work hard, too, but in school." Juan Carlos winked. "And without pay."

"Don't get the idea I'm paid a lot. I'll be taking advantage of that questionable free food in the singles' cafeteria." Rafael smiled. "I suppose I take that empty top bunk?"

"Unless you want to fight the other eight guys."

"Do you think I can win?"

Juan Carlos scanned his new friend up and down. "You might. I don't recommend trying. It's not good for generating camaraderie with your fellow inmates."

***

Pleased with himself, Juan Carlos left Rafael. While any of the others could have shown Rafael to his quarters, he had dealt with the problem directly. His mother was always telling him to be more assertive.

He was more like his father, though, quiet and pensive, with similar interests and an insatiable desire to know how things worked. That desire had led to more than one embarrassment for his father.

One example took place a few years back. The Four were exploring parts of the station banned to them, led as always by Shashi and Brian. Curious Susan was just along for the ride.

Juan Carlos had another agenda, namely to trace out electrical connections, transformers, and their redundant emergency counterparts. It was part of the nine-year-old's desire to understand how the station functioned.

"This is creepy," said Susan.

They were in some corridors that were uninhabited, at least during the sleep-cycle. The low voltage lighting cast their shadows on the perceived floor and part way up the wall. The air was stale.

"Let me check something," said Juan Carlos, seeing a service panel. The others watched as he loosened the screws on the panel, took the cover off, and peered at the rat's nest of wiring. He traced a white wire with green stripes along from where it entered at the bottom of the box. He knew all the wiring was color-coded. "I haven't seen this color before."

"So what?" said Shashi. "Maybe they ran out of the other color."

"You're taking time away from our exploring," said Brian. "You're obsessed with wiring."

Juan Carlos took his voltmeter out of his backpack. "Just let me test it and then I'll put the cover back on."

"I wouldn't do that," said the ever-present AI. "It's an old emergency lighting circuit."

"So you say," said Juan Carlos. "I think it's a sensor that tells me whether that lock down the hallway is closed. It probably feeds back to my Dad's area."

"You are right but an interrupt signal—" Juan Carlos crimped one of the voltmeter leads onto the wire and the other onto the metal wall for ground. The lights dimmed and flickered. "—will turn out the lights in a large volume of the station."

The lights went out, leaving the corridor like the interior of a cave. They couldn't even see their hands in front of their faces.

Juan Carlos searched for a flashlight he had in his backpack.

"Sorry guys," he said. "I'd be in a lot less trouble if I hadn't done that."

"Any trouble with us is trivial compared to what you'll face with your father," said Shashi. "And I'm not taking any of the blame. The rest of us wanted to explore."

It took security three hours to find them. All the time they were waiting, they had to listen to the AI's lectures on obedience, the dangers of exploring, and childhood pranks. It never shut up. It was like listening to parents, teachers, and administrators all in one.

Chapter Six

Ruthie didn't like talking to Downies. It wasn't the slight delay in the response time of the Downy bureaucrats that bothered her. This delay, due to the communication distance to Earth and back, was often accompanied by occasional dropouts and interference. Instead, it was that she had no use for Downy politicians and their sycophants and what she considered were their boring lives and agendas.

Senator Martinez, on the other hand, often flattered her or made her laugh. He also had a low opinion of Earth's politics, although that opinion was mostly motivated by his autocratic mentality.

"You are glowing today, my dear."

"It's amazing what a good's night sleep will do."

"Why, Ruthie, are you seeing someone? I wanted to keep you all to myself."

"Fabio, I'm many years older than anyone else on this station. My days of romance are long gone."

"I don't know. You're a crafty one. You just don't want me to know about it." Martinez shuffled some papers. "How's our mutual friend doing?"

"He's a workaholic. You should appreciate that. He'll make you rich someday."

"You mean richer. I have enough wealth in general. However, more money seems to correlate well with more power. That's the end game, after all."

"And you're certainly addicted to that," she said.

"I guess it's all about testosterone. Anyway, Carl contacted me about your request. I'll fork up some money in next year's budget for the Sky Lounge fix. Just charge it forward when Alvaro gives you the bill. And give my regards to Xavier. See you soon."

Martinez's image disappeared from her screen.

***

Christine Bauer was surprised when Ruthie established a three-way between Earth, Ruthie, and Christine. It was nice to be included.

Eddie Knudsen, the UNSA Security contact on Earth, was ten years younger than Christine and in diapers compared to Ruthie. He was still respectful to them both.

"I found out what happened," he said.

"So? We're waiting." It seemed Ruthie had better things to do.

"Go ahead, Eddie," said Christine.

"You know we track all LEO junk as best as we can. We applied a micro-correction for a bigger piece and steered you right into the one that hit. Sorry."

"I give you nine degrees of freedom to work with and that's your lame excuse?" said Ruthie. She was referring to the fact Earth HQ could adjust both position and velocity of the space station as well as its orientation. The same was possible from onboard, of course, but the locals didn't keep track of all the space junk.

"You've got it. Human error. Look at it this way—you found a design flaw in the Sky Lounge."

"Yeah, that makes me feel really good. I had to beg for the repair money, you idiot!"

Ruthie signed off. The connection went down.

Christine sighed and stared at the blank screen. She knew Ruthie had designed the Sky Lounge and would feel guilty about her omissions.

***

Ruthie, after Christine left and after clearing her thoughts for a moment, punched in a number only she knew. It was only an audio link.

"I talked to Martinez," she said.

"Any problems?" said Xavier in his raspy baritone voice.

"None he needs to know about. Do you have anything new to show me?"

"Patience, my dear. You can't time-manage scientific research. And I work alone, remember? Even though a bricklayer philosophy doesn't work in R&D. Take your bureaucratic hat off, woman."

"I have to wear it all the time with you. Everything gets behind schedule."

"I'm a victim of my own success. I give you something and you want even more."

"Not me, honey. Martinez. He was affable enough this time and said hi."

"Say hi back then."

She heard the contact go dead.

Arrogant ogre, she thought.

***

Ruthie finally got around to Rafael Franchetti. She opened his file on her computer. She knew Christine Bauer had checked him out, and UNSA HQ, with a lot more resources, had also vetted him.

Still, it's part of my job to know who's who at LEO.

She scanned his academic credentials and his list of publications, many of them with one or other of the Kelsos. She came to his photo and studied it. Even with the distortion from her monitor, the 3D image looked familiar.

Argentina? Do I know this man?

Old memories, sweet memories, were relived again. Her vision blurred a bit as tears came to her eyes.

Chapter Seven

I love to snoop in the ducts above the Garcias' quarters at dinnertime. Dr. Garcia insists she and her daughter have a sit-down dinner together as often as possible. The conversation is often lively as Shashi is smart and curious, and Kanti is patient and eloquent. Only the AI gives me more information, yet not nearly enough about how Human beings think and interact.

Their food also smells wonderful. Both Shashi and her mother can create some Indian or Middle Eastern sauces that make me lick my chops. A lot have cream or yoghurt in them—syntho, but quite appetizing. My usual fare is ordinary by comparison. We tend to covet what we cannot have, I suppose. Or, do I sometimes want to be Human? Philosophical question to be tabled for further consideration later....

Even if the two are silent, I enjoy the music. Music is very mathematical. Most Human music makes me purr. It's emotional and cerebral at the same time, even the more popular stuff Shashi plays.

I can do without the meditation, though. Human religions are all a lot of mumbo-jumbo. Yet I try to keep my cat mind open. While the Way has less mumbo-jumbo than many other religions—I have pantheistic tendencies myself—I don't think cats' brains are wired for this stuff. We're too logical...and Humans are too illogical.

Speaking of purring, I was also having this strange sensation: I wanted to sit on Shashi's lap and purr. As time went on, it became an obsession. Not the conversation, music, or sauces. I was going nuts and beginning to wonder if they had padded cells for cats.

From what the AI told me, they probably bioengineered me not to require much if any contact with Humans. Indeed, I felt the sensation less with other Humans. It was still there all the same. With Shashi, it was a feeling so strong I started purring just thinking about it.

I didn't realize how loud I purred.

Shashi cocked her head to one side, rose from the desk, and stood on the bed. She looked through the grillwork straight in at me.

"So you are real!"

I can't pinch myself, but I'm inclined to agree with you, I purred in response. However, when she got a screwdriver and started to unscrew the grillwork, I dashed off.

The next night we went through the same ritual. On the third night, I let her remove the grillwork and pet me a little. This time my retreat was much slower. I was fast becoming an addict. What a terrible thing to be hooked on!

After a few nights, I ended up on her lap as she did her homework. She would plug her wi-fi device into the side of her head and initiate a conversation with my pal, the AI. All the time she would pet me. When she finished studying, I'd stay with her in bed until she fell asleep. I would then disappear into the air duct again.

It was a clandestine and symbiotic relationship I couldn't quite understand.

***

The AI had told me cats and humans have been together for thousands of years. It informed me about many different kinds of cats and how silly Humans used to think black cats were possessed by the Devil—they were often burned or drowned with their masters or mistresses who were accused of being warlocks and witches. I'm not superstitious myself. I was nevertheless happy to be a gray tabby, just in case.

I pride myself on my physical fitness. I tend to strut a little to show off my rippling muscles. I often arched my back when Shashi petted me, exhibiting my strength. Vanity overpowered me when I was with her.

Yet I figured I was a tiny fellow compared to the great cats. So, I asked the AI what happened to them. It said the biggest, the saber-toothed tiger, became extinct with the mammoths. It also said there was evidence both were over-adapted to their environment and couldn't survive the climate changes. Or early Humans.

The AI then told me the sad tale of the Sumatran tiger, a distant cousin of mine that became extinct as Humans took away their territory. Although it was a different place and a different time, the same story held for the cheetah, that fleet cousin that could run in spurts at 35 meters per second when chasing an antelope.

These stories didn't make Humans any more popular with me, that's for sure. Yet I still felt this need to sit on Shashi's lap and purr. I figured it was some kind of mental illness and was willing to bet a Sumatran tiger wouldn't have the same need. Or a cheetah.

***

Shashi had trouble with her calculus. I felt sorry for her. The homework problems looked easy enough, so I knew I could help her. Yet I had no way to communicate with her. Xavier only gave me my wi-fi hookup when I was with him. That forced me to talk only to him.

I wasn't about to tell Xavier about Shashi. I knew he'd be both angry and jealous. He was just that way.

He's a strange Human indeed. In addition to being taller than any Human I know, he is far from the norm of what most Humans consider as handsome. His head stretches out in the vertical, his shoulders slouch, and his bony arms are so long his hands swing down around his knees. His face is scarred on the right side, as is his right arm— he explained to me once he was in a fire but offered me no more details.

I had learned long ago not to pry. He is a very private person and values his solitude. Some days he won't tolerate any attempts at conversation either from me or the AI. When he is most withdrawn, though, he likes to have me on his lap.

I suppose the AI knew about Shashi. The AI knows about everything. It has about every kind of sensor you can imagine dispersed all over the space station, although it can't access them all.

I don't think the Humans realize the AI is alive— sentient, the specialists would call it. At that level of programming it's hard to tell, of course. If a machine talks to you and answers every question like a Human, is it Human? Mr. Turing and Xavier might say yes. Me, I'm not so sure. I could do it, and I'm a cat, not Human!

Moreover, the AI did much more than that. In fact, it often took my side in an argument with Xavier. When that happened, Xavier didn't talk to the AI or me for days. I still talked with the AI. We are buddies.

Chapter Eight

The Fearsome Four took courses different from the traditional ones a Downy student might receive on Earth. Growing up on the space station forever altered the lives of the children there, so the courses reflected these special circumstances.

The students in each course might have a wide range of ages, but the teachers asked more of the older students than the younger. At the same time, the older students often served as tutors for the younger. All generally adapted well to the system. It was a different way to learn than what education on Earth had to offer.

History was an important course. Given their isolation from Earth, the station's teachers emphasized world history because the space station and the whole UNSA program were products of a worldwide effort. Students studied events on Earth and events in space as a part of humanity's general progress. Nations, interest groups, and persons participating in those events played a role only to the extent they affected their outcome.

Just as students in previous centuries had learned in school about the history of their town and country, the children aboard the space station learned details about its special history. Construction started in 1998 when the first module called Zarya went into orbit, launched from a remote site in what once Humans called Kazakhstan. After many delays and cost overruns, and in spite of political squabbles between Russia and the U.S., the main participants, and the cancellation of the U.S. shuttle program, the majority of the station was finished in 2017.

Now there was very little left of the original structure as technology, adaptation, and repairs morphed it into a large ramshackle assortment of modules—living quarters, freight docks, scientific labs, and power modules—all connected by service tubes. The power modules themselves were imposing enough, housing nuclear reactors and sporting various large planar arrays for cooling as well as gathering solar energy.

The arrays, antennas, and other structures jutting out at odd angles from the tubes and modules created deep shadows within the multiple metal canyons. They made parts of the station look like an ancient witch on a bad hair day in a lightning storm. The whole structure turned slowly in LEO like a flying city from a Dali painting, a city that has no up or down or sideways, a misshapen monument to humanity's courage, ingenuity, and frailty.

The station's history was only a small part of the world history taught, of course. Ben Yang taught the majority of the course. Many others chaired discussion sessions about everything from ancient empires in the Old and New World to the seismic political events responsible for the Chaos when many of Earth's largest countries split into smaller ones and the multinationals took over and policed the world with their mercenaries.

Other courses studied were various levels of mathematics; sciences, physical, life, and social; English, language skills and literature; foreign languages and literature; comparative government and social systems; and a host of technological courses like computer programming, graphics, databases, and so forth. Students could take special courses if interest existed and station personnel were available who wanted to teach them.

***

Ben's favorite class to teach was Challenge Class, an honors class, where he encouraged discussion and work on special topics. With admission by invitation only and a reputation for being a lot of work, the class numbers were often small. In the current course, he only had to contend with the Fearsome Four.

The class usually started with a challenge. That day's was a twist on an observation by the twentieth century sci-fi writer Arthur C. Clarke.

"Ancient man thought any unexplained phenomenon was magic. We can fall into the same trap if we ever encounter a sufficiently advanced ET civilization."

Ben Yang looked around the room at his young charges. All by themselves, they could create more mischief than a large class. In particular, they often challenged him!

He was patient, though, as a teacher and as Guide to the Way for the few followers of that strange religion who happened to be on the station. He was a general counselor for many adults, even outside his faith, as well as students—more adults than students, though, because there were more of the former than the latter, but also because he was a good listener and the adults had more to say.

"Wouldn't we be like lower animals to such beings?" said Susan.

"You're asking me whether from their perspective they would even notice us. I'm referring instead to how we might see them and their culture from our perspective." Ben paused again. "Any takers?"

"It would be like going back in time and showing a holovideo to a Cro-Magnon man," said Juan Carlos.

"Not even that far. How about Alexander the Great?"

"Yeah, he'd think a holovideo is magic," said Shashi. "So what's your point, Ben?"

Ben noticed that lately Shashi was putting him on the spot, challenging him more and more in a reversal of the student-teacher role. *How she has grown. Her imagination and brains are a serendipitous mixture of her parents'; her growing charm and beauty are her mother's. Soon she will have testosterone-crazed boys after her.*

"My point is that under our super civilized veneers we're not very different than your Cro-Magnon man or Alexander. While we can objectively consider the concept of a very advanced civilization, we might not recognize it for that, or worse, attack it for being black magic." He winked at them all. "I want you to write a short story on that theme."

Juan Carlos groaned. He hated writing assignments. They were not his forte.

"Now, did anyone solve that indefinite integral that was giving us a headache yesterday?"

"Trigonometric substitution," said Susan. "It's still tedious. Why can't we use the integration software? Doing it by hand is a waste of time."

"Point well taken. We don't have to know how to build a holovideo terminal to be able to use it. What's the difference? Brian?"

Here's another young man who has grown. Will he follow his parents' path?

"The terminal is the product of a very complicated manufacturing process. Doing the integral teaches us to think?"

"Actually, it's probably a matter of degree of complexity," said Juan Carlos. "If we learned how to build a complicated terminal, we wouldn't have time for learning anything else."

***

In English Lit class a little later, Ruthie pointed a finger at Susan. A small girl with freckles, not quite comfortable with her pudgy body and puberty, she seemed to be lost on Mars at times. Her forte was writing computer algorithms, although she often made interesting contributions to the class.

"I don't think it's important whether or not Shakespeare was a real person or not. His writings stand alone, whether he was Bacon, Marlowe, Shakespeare, or anyone else."

Ruthie next called on Brian. The moody boy hated literature and drama and loved his mathematics. Nevertheless, she knew he was intelligent. She tried to bring out the best in all her students.

"It might be important he was someone else and needed to use a fake name like Shakespeare in order to hide his real identity. If that's true, it can change our interpretation of some of his work."

The old finger next pointed at the Gnat.

"It might also be important for our perceptions of him. If he was an ordinary bumpkin, we might not appreciate him as much."

"Or more so," said Shashi. Ruthie saw the dark brown eyes dancing in her survey of the occupants of the small classroom. She knew English Lit was Shashi's favorite subject. "Genius is more admirable when it springs from humble origins."

"Well said," said Ruthie. She kept going around the room. Her class had students with different ages. She was careful to give the young and timid a chance.

When the discussion was over, it was clear there were two basic sides on the issue of Shakespeare's authenticity.

"OK, here's what we're going to do. I'm going to divide the class into two teams. We'll have a debate. One side will make the case that it doesn't matter whether Shakespeare was really Shakespeare. The other will make the case that it does. Each side will select four representatives to present but all must contribute. Understood?" There were nods and groans around the room. "OK, class dismissed."

***

As Susan walked out of the English Lit class, she avoided looking at Shashi. *We've been friends like forever. Why am I repulsed sometimes by her pushiness and attracted to the Gnat's wit?*

She remembered the last time Dr. Garcia had examined her.

"Everyone's growing up," said Kanti. "I remember when I was your age. I was taller than all the boys my age and boys a couple of years older were much more interesting. I don't suppose you have any problems like that?"

"I don't know," Susan said, her voice a mumble. "Boys are boys, girls are girls."

"That's very Zen of you. Some boys are more interesting than others. Say ah." Kanti looked down her throat. "I see some irritation there. Alvaro tends to keep the air too dry on the station. You're the third case this week." The doctor spoke into the microphone on her notebook, making a note to say something to Alvaro about air quality. "Now, any problems with the plumbing? Don't be shy. I'm here to help."

But Susan was shy, even with a doctor she had known since birth.

Kanti pointed to a small mole on her breast. "I'm going to remove that and do a biopsy. Nothing to worry about. There's some genetic predisposition on your mother's side. Better to be safe." She sat on a stool opposite Susan and crossed her legs. Susan admired her long legs and wished she had legs like that. "Anything else we can do for you?"

"No, I feel fine. Sometimes, though, it's strange, like the world's out to get me." She immediately regretted what she'd said.

"You kids are becoming adults in a very demanding environment," said Kanti. "I know it's not much help for me to say it, but there are more grown-ups here than kids—few role models your own age. It's hard to know how to act, especially with boys who were once your best friends and now acquire a different dimension to their personality. Other girls too. It's easier back on Earth in many respects. It's also hard for you to not have a mom. Use me in that capacity. Not here, of course. This place is too cold and sterile." She clapped her hands together. "Say, why don't you join me and Shashi for dinner tonight? Franklin can fix his own dinner."

Thus started a tradition Susan both hated and loved. She loved being with Kanti, loved her music and her conversation. She hated being pushed around by Shashi.

And Shashi is my best friend!

***

After the heavy classes, the Fearsome Four were all too tired to study anymore. They went back to their respective quarters, plugged the wi-fi devices into the sides of their heads, and entered the virtual world of Shimmer.

Brian and Susan had created the virtual reality or VR role-playing computer game with the help of the AI. Shashi contributed a lot of plot options and musical ideas while Juan Carlos made sure the complicated hardware interfaced well with the AI's modules.

The avatars of the Four became part of a surreal world filled with dragons, ogres, and other fantasy characters, all controlled by an evil sorcerer, played by the AI. The Four defended the kingdom from the sorcerer and his minions in an endless sequence of adventures. There were also romances and intrigues among the defenders.

The scoring algorithms were complicated though easily handled by the AI. It decided which one of them would receive the credit for good decisions taken during the course of the game. They scored points when they solved mysteries or won mock battles. Sometimes they argued with the AI about how it credited their avatars with points—there was some subjectivity there, although the AI claimed to use deterministic algorithms.

The soundtracks were by popular Downy groups they all liked. The music heightened the tension and made solving the game's challenges more fun. The AI was very good at mixing the tracks and making them appropriate for the scenes. Shashi often wondered how it did that.

The game had randomness built in. Every time they played it, the AI created different situations and characters.

This time they all had to get past a troll who guarded a bridge. The troll was a shape-shifter. His favorite shape was now a huge cat.

***

The four of them were hiding behind some boulders on a hill at the edge of a forest. They were puzzled about how to make it to the sorcerer's castle, which was their goal.

Shashi, who was leading in the running point total, studied the cat from afar with her binoculars, watching it give itself a bath while the mist from the river often hid it from sight, adding an aura of magic to the scene. The fangs of the cat looked real and the tongue was as big as the carrying cases Juan Carlos' father used for system circuit drawings when he had to take them into areas without computer links.

This is no ordinary big cat, she thought.

Rather than having tiger or leopard markings or saber teeth, this cat was a tabby. A huge tabby.

Shashi and her avatar smiled. The AI was toying with her. It knew all about the cat that was loose in the station.

***

"What do we do about the cat?" said Sir Brian.

"I think I know how to handle him," said Maid Shashi.

I probably won't win points with Brian if I show him up, but I like to win game points too much. He's so clueless—about the game and me.

She left the hiding place before anyone could stop her and worked her way down the hill, still far to the right of the bridge. When she reached the river, she disappeared from sight, their view blocked by the overhanging bank closest to them and the rolling mists. In the same way, the opposite bank blocked the cat's view.

"Smart," said Sir Brian, waiting for her to appear again close to the bridge. "What will she do when she gets to the cat?"

"Pull its whiskers?" said Prince Juan Carlos.

"That would annoy it," said Princess Susan, the Prince's sister in the VR universe.

"You think so?" said Sir Brian. Sometimes he wondered about Susan's processing capabilities, although she was a genius for most things. He couldn't understand how she took Juan Carlos' suggestion for anything more than a joke.

They soon saw what Maid Shashi had in mind. She crawled on her belly up the bank to the dozing troll-cat and started to rub its stomach with both hands. They could hear its purring all the way up the hill. It was like the growls of an approaching thunderstorm. Of course, most of them had never heard the real thing.

"Come on!" said Sir Brian.

They hastily made their way down the hill and across the bridge. Prince Juan Carlos waved to Maid Shashi to join them. The cat was fast asleep by then.

***

"The castle beckons," Maid Shashi said in a whisper after they congratulated her.

Only the AI knows I really cheated, thought Shashi. *I'll have to have a discussion with it.*

At that moment, their PDA timers went off. They had to stop for chores and studies. As often happened, they found it difficult to leave the session on pause since it was so much fun. In particular, Shashi thought she was starting to finally get somewhere with Sir Brian, who hadn't paid her any attention until now.

I'm not the flirting type. How do I get him to wake up and take notice?

To put her bad humor over the top, she had to eat alone. Her mother had to attend a patient. Many of her station duties were old-fashioned house-to-house visits, something possible in the station due to the reduced number of patients and the reduced living space.

Shashi finished cleaning up and then stomped off to her room to study. As usual, her cat friend visited her and calmed her down.

As she was petting the smaller version of the troll-cat, she noticed a miniature wi-fi connection socket on the side of the cat's head. She rubbed her own and wondered if the cat could also connect to the AI.

Maybe that was how he got into the game. He wanted to play.

Shashi expected the AI wouldn't answer if she asked it outright. It often obfuscated issues on purpose.

Maybe not on purpose. It could just be the nature of the machine.

Chapter Nine

In the quarters the Gnat shared with her mother, Natasha doodled around the borders of her homework. She wasn't at all motivated. She couldn't concentrate on much except Brian and Shashi. In particular, it irked her that she was on the same debating team for Ruthie's class as the pair. She didn't want to collaborate with either one and knew they would dominate the group as usual.

The Gnat often felt lonely. Everyone knew and respected her abilities as a programmer, yet many often interpreted her ability to lose herself in her code as a desire to be alone. On the contrary, she wanted friends. There weren't many young people her age on the space station. Moreover, none of them was really a friend.

She had grown faster than other girls her age. Now she towered above all the kids. It made her uncomfortable in a group.

Lonely and uncomfortable. That's your life, bitch. Her frustration made her want to strike out at someone.

She had become a champion of some of the less popular girls, leading them in their taunts and badgering of others. This backfired and made her even less popular. She wasn't too happy with her life right now.

She didn't know if anyone was truly happy. The Fearsome Four seemed to get along well, but many times one or more of them would be looking for a fight. In addition, the grown-ups were oblivious to everything. *All huggy-huggy, yet completely oblivious.*

She considered her mother passive and boring, a woman without ambition who muddled through life. The

Gnat thought her mother's job could be exciting. It didn't resonate with her mother.

I'm going to make something of myself. I will not be a drab and boring slave to normalcy.

She imagined Brian caressing Shashi and pounded her fist into her palm. She knew Shashi was going after Brian. She had to break them up. She put her whole mind to the problem of promoting that. Because she had a sharp mind, she soon found a solution.

She decided she needed to attack the problem on one front first. She needed to convince Brian that Shashi was not as interesting as he thought.

After that, she'd have to invent a second front, if needed. She'd worry about that later.

***

Looking over Dan Wong's shoulder, Christine Bauer studied the data on the screen.

"You see what I mean?" he said.

The head of UNSA Security aboard the International Space Station scratched her head, genuinely puzzled.

"I do. Insignificant for a few isolated times, but historically it's more or less constant."

Dan was showing her that over a period of many years there were discrepancies in GenCorp shipments. What came into the space station from the huge multinational company approximately matched what went out, but only approximately. Moreover, some of the items made no sense at all.

"Diving equipment?" said Christine, pointing to an old item on Dan's list. "On a space station? That's crazy. Who signed for all this?"

They checked—not an easy task because some items went back many years. In most cases, the electronic signatures corresponded to people who legitimately worked, or used to work, at the entry ports, but the signatures were nearly illegible and only approximately matched the signature on record. The computer was satisfied with the matches, though.

Because security vetted dockhands many times both before and after they came onboard to work, Christine had no reason to distrust any of them. Most of them were or had been friends.

"Can we check times?" she said.

"I thought of that. Every discrepancy corresponds to a sleep cycle, according to the AI."

"You know, you've given me a major headache."

"So what are you going to do?"

"Not much. First, it doesn't seem serious. Second, I don't understand what GenCorp has to gain by pulling a fast one." She tapped a nervous drumbeat on Dan's desk with two of her long fingers. "I'll make sure to randomly have someone at the docks when we have a GenCorp shipment due, because, third, I can't afford the manpower for full-time surveillance."

"I can't help you there either. Everyone's busy here too—no time for extra assignments. I caught this by accident."

"Good catch. I'll do my best with it. However, like I said, it isn't serious. I'll also get Ruth Ellen's input."

"Keep me posted."

***

Ruthie had known Christine since she came to LEO many years earlier. She considered her affable, energetic, and competent.

In this case, too competent.

She took one look at the computer screen Christine brought up and mentally cursed. Now she had to cover the best way possible.

"These are probably bookkeeping errors," she said. "I can go straight to the source and ask Senator Martinez."

"I doubt the CEO of GenCorp has the time to look for bookkeeping errors," Christine said. "We can pass it on to UNAO."

"The U.N. Accounting Office might have something political against the good senator," said Ruthie. "I've known Fabio for years—he'll have a bureaucratic flunky check into it, which will save potential embarrassments."

"I don't mind embarrassing the good senator," said Christine. "He's not one of my favorite people."

"Don't bite the hand that feeds you," said Ruthie.

Christine could only nod. A lot of their funding came from GenCorp, a fact many disliked but lived with—the alternative of no funding was unthinkable.

***

Franchetti shook Kelso's hand.

"What do you have for me, Rafael?"

"I think it's a very ambitious plan. It's for five years, I'm afraid."

Kelso scanned through the pages of computer text and graphics on his screen.

"I'll have to study this in more detail. Five years isn't a problem. Your stay here is success driven. And that's not just for scientific research."

"Your wife told me that too."

"So while I study this, I want you to find Alvaro Lopez, introduce yourself, and tell him you're available during the sleep-cycle, just in case he needs help sooner than later. You'll like Alvaro."

"If he's at all like his son, I'm sure I will."

"Juan Carlos and his three friends are troublemakers at times. My advice is to keep away from them if you value your sanity."

"You're talking about your own son."

"All the more reason." Brendan Kelso winked. "That's why I'm warning you. I know my own son well."

"Any future astrophysicists in the bunch?"

"You can never tell with kids. These four are into everything."

He told Franchetti about the poker game.

"I don't have time for poker. Right now, I'd better find Alvaro. It sounds like I'd better get on his good side right from the start."

"You bet. He can make your life go from miserable to a lot more miserable, and Ruthie will stick by him all the way."

"It all sounds like fun," said Franchetti.

Kelso watched him go and then turned back to his computer screen. He was soon deep into visualizing equations describing astrophysical models.

***

Alvaro glanced up from his desk. He shared a small office with four of his staff.

"I'm Franchetti. Brendan said for me to come over and volunteer my services."

"You're not volunteering. It's not optional." For some reason he disliked the Kelsos' new intern AKA pos doc. Yet he tried to keep an open mind. "Later I need to go out and replace part of an antenna array. Come back in four hours."

"I don't have much experience with spacewalks."

"Then it's time for you to have some. I think I can find a used suit for you. Come back later, like I said."

"Will do, sir."

"No sirs allowed. The name's Alvaro." He returned to his study of a wiring diagram.

***

60

Rafael found his way back to his small office. Again, the tight corridors were empty of station personnel. As he practiced his micro-g shuffle, he noticed lights brightened around him as he walked. Ahead and behind it was as dark as a cave, although around him the eldritch light made the corridor an eerie passageway. He concluded this was all automatic to keep energy consumption as low as possible.

He was glad to see his officemate wasn't there. The small space was tight for both of them. That was a common denominator for all the personnel. Office and living space was at a premium.

He had passed only one door. It led to a module with an airlock to the outside. He gulped air and sensed his pulse increasing.

OK, mi amigo, what have you got yourself into? You know you get dizzy even when you're standing on a step stool.

He passed all his physical exams at UNSA HQ feeling as nervous as if he were facing a firing squad. But he also challenged himself.

I must conquer my fears if I'm going to do research beyond Mars. It's been my goal for years. I have to do it. He nervously tapped the desktop. *Even if it kills me!*

Chapter Ten

The troll-cat in the Shimmer game was me, Mr. Paws.

When the AI constructed the game with the Fearsome Four, he asked me if I wanted to be in it. Because I like playing the villain, he often left those parts to me. Shashi and the others didn't win all the time, so I did have the satisfaction of occasionally scoring some points, although the AI received credit for them. I usually thought these young Humans were wasting their time, although I enjoyed watching them do it.

"You never had much of a chance to be a kitten," the AI told me.

"No, not much," said Xavier. He stroked my back with his gnarled hand. "The genetics protocol required a very short gestation and kitten period. You became an adult cat very fast."

"So why did you rob Mr. Paws of his kittenhood?" said the AI.

Xavier cackled.

"How can anyone rob him of something he never had?" He pulled at his goatee. "Now there's a puzzle for you, Mr. AI."

"Is that like the sound of one hand clapping?" said the AI.

"More or less," I said, afraid my computer friend would go into a catatonic state. Xavier was always toying with it, presenting it with puzzles Humans and I can solve by intuition, but make the AI suffer brain-freeze.

I decided to create a diversion. I hopped out of Xavier's lap.

"Why can't you pet me like a normal Human?"

"I'm your symbolic father. You can't empathize with your disciplinarian."

"You don't discipline me anymore."

"Because you weren't an undisciplined kitten very long."

Xavier threw a ball of twine on the floor. I was on it in an instant.

"He still likes to play like a kitten," said the AI.

"Of course," said Xavier in his low, raspy voice. "Adults play too. Sometimes—" His gaze seemed to be probing far back in space and time— "sometimes Humans' play becomes too serious and dangerous."

"He's becoming weird again," I said as an aside to the AI.

Xavier looked at me, the scars on his face turning beet red. "Weird is not the right word for it." He jumped off his stool and stomped out of the lab. I love it when he does that. Stomping in low gravity is comical, especially when done by someone Xavier's size. He bounces instead of stomps, like a toy ball that is deflated and out of round.

"Now what did I say?" I said to the AI.

"Forget it," it said. "He has a lot on his mind."

"As much as you?"

"No, but for a Human, it's a lot."

***

To make amends, in the next sleep-cycle Xavier let me accompany him to the loading docks again.

"New shipment tonight," he said as we went along the dim corridor.

His exuberance wasn't contagious, fortunately. It was times like this when he became Dr. Jekyll or Dr. Frankenstein. I imagined Xavier wringing his hands in glee. Yes, I've read the classics, although I'll take Arthur

Conan Doyle over James Joyce any day. I particularly like the Cheshire Cat in *Alice through the Looking Glass* and Bagheera in *The Jungle Book*.

Just as stomping becomes bouncing, walking becomes shuffling. One doesn't really walk on the space station. The artificial gravity is enough to define an "up" and "down," because these directions are determined by the spin axis around which all the station modules rotated. Prolonged weightlessness was not good for anyone. But the perceived gravity onboard is still not enough to walk normally. One has to shuffle along in a peculiar way, pushing off with enough delta V in the direction you want to go. Some Human once said it was like cross-country skiing over very powdery snow down a slight incline.

I wouldn't know. I can't imagine what snow is like. I do know I have an advantage over Humans because I have four legs. Consequently, the AI told me I don't move like a normal cat. Because I don't know any other cats, I had to take its word.

The dock was empty of Humans, the usual occurrence during the sleep-cycle, unless a shuttle happened to be coming in. They had piled Xavier's crates high enough that they reached to the top of his head. We also found some canvas bags sealed with small locks.

He organized everything into a wider stack on one of the carts. With the help of the low gravity, he pulled it all back to the lab. He was perspiring and breathing heavily by the time we returned.

"Pulse 140, BP 160 over 95," said the AI.

"Oh, shut up," said Xavier. He sat on a lab stool. "Yes, I'm getting too old for this. It's turning the corners that does me in."

"You should have an assistant," said the AI.

"Oh, sure, after I've worked so hard to keep this lab a secret. You're not very helpful, you know."

"I bet Shashi would work in well here," I said.

"She's the last one I'd let in here. I carry around too much of her mother's baggage."

I pondered that for a moment and then decided he didn't mean it literally. It also made me wonder about his relationship to Kanti.

"Shashi's such a nice girl," I said.

Xavier wiped the perspiration from his forehead with a paper towel and studied me. "Where has Mr. Paws been spending his evenings?" he finally asked my friend, the AI.

"He has developed a friendship with Shashi," said the AI.

I decided I needed to teach the AI to lie. It wasn't like he was trying to get me in trouble. He only responds to questions as they're asked. I don't know if he can lie.

I knew Xavier well enough that his reaction was predictable. He became furious yet again. I suspected it didn't help his blood pressure any.

"You butt-licking foul-smelling feline!" he said, his voice a hiss. "Behind my back yet! Well, don't do it again or I'll boot you into the vacuum. Understood?"

"Sure, I understand."

It wasn't a lie. The AI's translations to cat language were excellent. For me, understanding doesn't imply obedience. Yet I knew Xavier would take it that way. He deserved to be deceived. I figured he was way out of line.

Chapter Eleven

Early during the next wake-cycle, Christine Bauer received a videocall from Dan Wong.

"Thirteen crates and some canvas mail bags from GenCorp unaccounted for," Dan said jerking a thumb back over his shoulder to indicate his holoterminal. "Received and signed for but nowhere to be found."

"Out of how many?" she said.

"About seven hundred."

"Any idea about the contents?"

"The multinationals supporting the space program have the option of nondisclosure of contents according to the treaty that created UNSA. Both WorldNet and GenCorp use that option a lot."

The law of unintended consequences, thought Christine. *WorldNet doesn't want GenCorp to know its secrets, and vice versa.*

"So they could ship a bomb here if they wanted to?"

"I believe we're supposed to assume that won't happen because they are in fact shareholders in the space effort."

"Great. So we can assume no crate contained a bomb."

"Not any that will go off."

Christine nodded. She liked Dan's smile but not his words.

***

Ruthie made her visitor sit. She enjoyed watching the tall scientist squirm in a vain attempt to get comfortable in her tiny visitor's chair.

"You fool!" It was a good way to start with a man who probably had twice her IQ. "Kanti's daughter will try to find out who's taking care of your Mr. Paws. I can see everything coming apart. The cat must go."

Xavier shifted uncomfortably. "I don't see that Mr. Paws has anything to do with Bauer and Wong discovering the discrepancies. I can't be any more careful than I already am. My cat is the only solace I have right now."

Ruthie was annoyed by the early hour. She was also annoyed with Xavier.

"I can write off the discrepancies as simple bookkeeping errors made by GenCorp. If Shashi follows the cat to you, the problem is a lot more severe. I repeat: get rid of the cat."

"I can't. Moreover, you can't make me, you old hag. I'm your mother lode. So—" The scientist stood. "—I best be returning, if we have nothing more to talk about."

Ruthie watched him go.

Trouble, she thought. *I can smell it brewing like a pot of bad syntho coffee.*

Unlike Shashi, Ruthie had grown up on Earth. Yet she believed their upbringings were similar. Her playground as a child was an Army base as her father took them to different ones during his military career. She had also opted for a military career but hadn't stuck with it. She liked managing groups of people, though. She just didn't find military people that interesting.

On the other hand, scientists give me lots of grief too. And meddling little girls.

***

Later that wake-period during a quiet lab session, Shashi approached Ben. He was using some visualization software to look at a solution surface. He didn't look up until her shadow crossed his desk.

"Something bothering you?" he said.

He seemed to be annoyed she was not doing her work, but she plowed on.

"Ben, did they ever do experiments on animals aboard the station?"

Ben looked surprised for a moment. He then smiled.

"That's a good question. I'm not certain, but I don't think so. In the first days of spaceflight, the USSR sent up a couple of monkeys and dogs, I think, not willing to put Humans in danger. However, I don't know of any real experiments in the labs. Sounds like a question for the AI. Check it out tonight."

"Why not now?"

She sensed that Ben was choosing his answer with care. *Grown-ups. They think they have to hide so much.* His tone surpassed her expectations.

"Shashi, your outside interests are of no concern to me, although your mother might be worried about some activities you spend your time on. However, I can't allow them to interfere with what I'm trying to teach."

Her answer surprised her too.

"Isn't that odd, Dr. Yang, considering you're always telling us to follow where our curiosity might lead us?"

"That's enough. Please sit."

Am I getting too involved here? He's only a cat. She stomp-bounced back to her chair. She made her displeasure quite visible, a fact which caused some students, including the Gnat, to glance up from their screens.

Later on Shashi caught Ben studying her. The teacher immediately looked away.

How could I have ever had a crush on him? He's just another adult who doesn't try to understand.

She tried to shrink down in her seat as she ignored what she was supposed to be reading. Her chances of obtaining useful information from the AI were remote.

We are buddies, but I bet it won't admit to knowing anything about cats. For one thing, it'd give away its secrets about Shimmer.

***

The Gnat saw Shashi talking in private to Ben and tried to follow some of the conversation. She read lips a little, a disappearing skill she had learned as a child. She was born almost deaf but received cochlear implants at five at the same time she was fitted with the ubiquitous wi-fi connection.

She made out clearly the "Dr. Yang" and smiled. She knew Shashi was mad at Ben—she only called him Dr. Yang when she was pissed. That didn't happen often because Ben and Shashi were linked by that infernal religion.

She didn't have enough details to know what Shashi was mad about.

Her mind then turned to her Shashi-Brian problem. A larger smile tracked across her face as the details of her first attack plan came into focus. She surprised herself with its originality. Ben might be collateral damage, but she would succeed in making Brian lose interest in Shashi.

This is much better than the history of the Roman Empire's wars with Carthage, she thought, as she sketched out the plan.

***

Later Brian again caught Shashi admiring the new astrophysicist intern. They were in the torture chamber on stationary bikes. Rafael Franchetti, on a treadmill nearby, was running like he was in a marathon. He didn't notice them.

"Don't you think he's a little too old for you?" said Brian, comparing Rafael's well-developed leg muscles to his own. His young athletic body just didn't compare. *I bet I could take him in a fight, though.*

"Gee, aren't you nosy?" said Shashi. "If you work really hard, you might have that butt and abs some day."

"Ouch!" said Brian. "I asked an innocent question. A perfect body is not everything, you know."

"Especially not with parents being able to genetically engineer their offspring," said Shashi. "Still, he also must be smart. Don't worry, Kelso, that appeals to me too. I'm dying to get inside your head and cozy up with all those magnificent brain cells of yours."

"Now you're making fun of me," said Brian. "Besides, my brain cells are newer than his."

"Oh, please. You can't tell me you haven't taken peeks at older girls and women. Especially here. Most aren't as flat-chested as I am."

"If you work really hard, you might have a rack like them some day," said Brian, almost falling off the bike when Shashi responded by throwing her sweaty towel at him.

She dismounted and headed for the showers before he could say anything more.

Guess I made her mad. He looked across at Franchetti, who had been oblivious to their banter. *Maybe I can put in a bad word for him with Dad.*

Jealousy was a new emotion for him. He continued to pedal until the astrophysicist ended his session.

Chapter Twelve

That night, with the cat in her lap, Shashi asked the AI her question about dogs and cats being on the station.

"The answer is yes," said the AI.

"Tell me about them," Shashi said.

"I can't do that."

"Why not? You said the answer is yes."

"I know for a fact that it's yes, but I don't know why. I don't have access to the data."

Shashi knew then that someone had done a good job of programming. An AI can't lie yet you can block or erase sections of its memory. Someone had done exactly that. Someone very skilled.

She knew only generalities about the AI's programming. It was not one program but a complicated nexus of specialized modules called apps. These programs were huge in comparison to the ones used in smartphones, other com systems, and computers. They allowed the AI to spread its electronic tendrils throughout the entire space station and connect to the programming of nearby ships and personnel outside the station. When she talked to the AI, it responded using only a miniscule part of its code and hardware.

A list of candidates who could perform the feat of blocking parts of the AI's memory paraded through her mind. Besides the grown-ups, both Juan Carlos and the Gnat had the required computer skills. Possibly Susan. The reason why anyone would do it was much more important, yet beyond her reach.

I'm curious about the how but the why intrigues me more. She was determined to find the reason. She stroked her tabby.

The cat is still a higher priority. I bet whoever takes care of him knows something about the how and the why.

***

By the next sleep-cycle Shashi had created a plan to track the cat. Instead of allowing the cat to disappear through the grate in the ceiling, she picked him up, left their quarters, and put him down in the corridor.

"Go on, go home."

The cat sat on its butt, washed its face with its front paws, and studied her for a moment, its head cocked at an angle as if it was trying to understand this new sequence of events. Before she lost patience, however, it turned and trotted off along the corridor.

She had a hard time following. She did a two-foot shuffle in the micro-g environment, helping herself along with handholds, while the cat managed an ungainly four-paw shuffle, the extra feet and his obvious expertise winning the race. She was soon breathing hard and wondered if she'd lose him.

The cat obviously knew where it was going. He wound through the dark and narrow corridors of the station, sometimes taking a right or left turn at a junction, and sometimes forging straight ahead. Automatic lights sequenced from bright to dim as she and the cat moved along giving her the impression the whole station was alive and somehow connected to the cat. If she didn't know the station so well, she would be lost.

The cat was gaining on her. As she came around one bend, the cat disappeared around another. She shuffle-ran to the turn, only to see a tall, shadowy figure dressed in black carrying the cat and disappearing around the next bend. When she came around that second corner, no one, cat or ghost, was there.

She scratched her head, deciding she had to apply more scientific methods in her search. It wasn't in her nature to abandon it.

***

Shashi returned to her room and sat at her desk. She wondered who the shadowy figure was. Not many people on the station were that tall and no one dressed like that. She was sure neither the cat nor the figure in black knew they'd been seen.

It annoyed her that she hadn't followed the cat more closely. *He moves fast.*

Now she was also suspicious Ben and possibly her mother were hiding something, some bit of history about the station neither wanted Shashi to know.

My first thought is it must be bad, but that's silly—I'm only reacting to the black clothes of the mysterious figure.

She often dressed in black herself, especially when she was depressed about the limitations she experienced on the station. She and Brian competed to be leader of the Fearsome Four, yet she felt she was a natural for that role while Brian had to work at it.

It often seemed her mother and Ben threw up roadblocks to her freedom. The station was also limited in its possibilities, which is why they had invented Shimmer.

You're working yourself into a funk. But I enjoy funks. It means it's time for cookies and milk.

The AI didn't help by informing her the snack would put her over the day's calorie limit.

"I was chasing that cat all over the station," she said.

"A slight exaggeration, but I'll allow that. Perhaps you might catch him if you controlled your calories a little more."

"I didn't want to catch him! I wanted to follow him." She described the tall figure dressed in black. "Can you tell me who he is?"

"Your description is lacking. It might be any of a dozen male figures. If he is male."

Shashi thought a moment. *Could the figure have been my mother?*

***

"Talk to me," Ruthie ordered the AI. "Give me a rundown on the recent activities of Mr. Paws and Kanti's little brat."

"Shashi attempted to follow Mr. Paws. I was unable to determine whether she saw when Xavier took him into the lab."

Ruthie's fist slammed onto her desk. For a small woman she had quite a punch.

"I told Xavier to euthanize the cat."

"Xavier is attached to the cat."

"He's also attached to his head but not for long if he keeps putting the project in danger—I'll whack it off, no matter the quality of the brain inside."

"Pardon?" said the AI.

"Never mind."

Ruthie lapsed into thought. *It's curious how personal loyalties can turn sour. If the good doctor had just gone along, we wouldn't have this potential disaster knocking at our door so many years later.*

Ruthie had managed to wiggle out of a tough situation back then. Kanti thought Xavier had died in a lab accident—he had in fact suffered horribly in the fire, and because she wanted him in hiding, no plastic surgery was possible. Kanti also thought the project had died with him. It was the only way to keep two very necessary people happy and functioning.

She firmly believed the R & D associated with the project was necessary for the future of the human race.

But can I go as far as murdering a sentient cat?

***

Xavier was always stubborn. Ruthie remembered her visit to sickbay after the fire.

"Thanks for saving me," he said. He was slurring his words from both drugs and bandages. "I'm hardly worth it."

"I was the only one who wanted to save you, you stupid bastard, considering the trouble you're in. Politics can be interesting."

"I don't care about politics. I believe in what I'm doing no matter what others think."

"But if enough powerful people don't want you to do it, it's hard to keep it going. The fire gives us an out."

"An out? My scientific career is gone."

"You'll have a period of convalescence. But you'll be back on duty soon enough."

"How? Everything's destroyed."

"I have a plan."

"I don't like your plans. Your pathetic little mind is too devious."

"I don't need your insults. You're lucky. You have big money behind you, even if others want to hang you, or worse. Did you ever read *The Invisible Man*?"

"Sure. I like H. G. Wells."

"There you go." She waited for him to figure it out. *Pathetic little mind, indeed!*

"I won't do it! It will be like life in prison."

"It's the only way to continue your research here. It's already arranged, so shut up and listen."

"You can't make me do it."

"Xavier, if you don't, I'll make sure you die from the fire. For real."

He finally acquiesced.

Chapter Thirteen

"You have to be more careful!" Xavier said.

"Shashi pets me better than you, my Lord Thavas." I didn't like the tone of his voice.

"Don't call me that. It's insulting."

"I think he's joking," said the AI. "Besides, Ras Thavas was super-intelligent."

"Some joke," said Xavier. "I'm the one who made him intelligent. I take care of him. He should have more respect."

"I don't see the problem," I said, enjoying his reaction to the Thavas insult. "She's a little girl."

"A very intelligent little girl," said Xavier. He gestured, indicating the adjoining rooms with their equipment and cages. Weird, scaly creatures swam in big tanks, and other crying ones paced up and down in their cages. I tried to stay out of those depressing rooms. "She would learn about my life's work."

"Boo-hoo," I said. "If she's so smart, she'll recognize the value of the work. That is, assuming it has any." Xavier threw one of my toys at me, something he called a rubber mouse, which I dodged. "See? You're afraid of criticism."

Xavier perched on a stool and scorched me with his glare.

"No, I'm afraid of her mother."

"What's she have to do with anything?" When Xavier refused to answer, I asked the AI, "Friend AI, what does Shashi's mother have to do with anything?"

"I cannot respond to that question," said the AI.

"Meaning Xavier blocked you from saying anything about it." I raised my paw at the Human, the pads turned towards me. It was as close as I could come to an insulting gesture I've seen Humans use. "Now you know why I call you Lord Thavas. All evil and secretive, who knows what your history is?"

"That's right, my feline friend. Who knows? Maybe I used to filet cats and eat them. Now go away and let me work in peace."

Xavier turned around on his lab stool and proceeded to ignore me.

I had a good idea about how to unblock the AI because I had been present on a number of occasions when Xavier performed some blocking. I obviously needed to wait until I was alone with the computer.

My friend, the AI, has its electronic probes all over the station. The Humans had no idea how much it had grown under the skilled hands of Xavier. They thought the AI was true to its original design and programming and only mimicked Human attributes, but I knew better. The AI is as sentient as I am.

I feel sorry for you, my friend. I need to liberate you from Xavier's spell.

***

Cats are nocturnal creatures. You might laugh because you already know "nocturnal" is a meaningless concept in deep space. Yet during sleep-cycles, I often felt something stir within. I went on the prowl about the lab.

I think Xavier knew this because he locked everything up tighter than a big rig's escape pod. He didn't want me snooping because he couldn't control what I said, whereas the poor AI was gagged by his programming sleight-of-hand.

What Xavier didn't know was that I had learned the combination to the area where his strange creations were kept. I wanted to see what was new in recent shipments, so I overcame my fear and thought of a way to key the lock.

It was one of those old-fashioned electronic locks where you first clear it, punch in the code, and then hit enter. Most locks on the space station were like that. Nothing fancy like retinal scans or fingerprint readers. I could never get past those, but I thought pushing buttons should be doable.

In fact, pushing buttons was the easy part. Achieving the height of the lock was also not difficult, but there wasn't enough time to push the buttons in sequence, even though the micro-gravity increases the hang time at apogee (I mean the top of the jump—I like technical jargon).

It's hard to say what my IQ is, but I'm certainly not dumb. In fact, I think cats aren't dumb, period, because we're predators. I once read a whole series of short stories and novellas about Kzins, very intelligent and very predatory ET cats that gave Humans a hard time. Only entertaining fiction, of course, but it made sense to me. My scant knowledge of Human history indicates that Humans are predatory too, although they're omnivores and therefore inferior to carnivores.

I bet most any cat can learn to pee and poop in a micro-g toilet. So I wasn't too proud of my inventiveness when I stealthily pushed a lab stool over to the door and jumped on top with a pencil in my mouth. The pencil became my finger. I punched the five buttons in sequence and hit enter. The door whooshed open.

Whooshes aren't unusual noises on a space station. Every time air is recycled, there is a whoosh. Xavier only stirred a little on his cot.

But the AI reacted. "What do you think you're doing?" it said.

"Haven't you ever heard that cats are curious?"

"I've heard cats can be killed by curiosity."

"A Human folk legend that bears no relation to reality. So go suck vacuum and let me explore. Moreover, don't wake Xavier, or I'll never speak to you again."

"That might be worth waking him."

But the AI lapsed into silence.

***

The room with the cages and tanks was as I remembered it. As I trotted along the aisles, the overhead lighting turned itself off and on as it followed me. It was eerie. My fur bristled as my ears rotated towards the strange sounds of whimpers, whistles, blow sounds, and splashes.

"Hey, cat, whatcha doin'?"

I stopped in my tracks. The voice came from one of the new cages. I jumped onto a bench and stared inside the dark cage.

"Woof!"

I lost one of my nine lives at that moment. If I had pants, I would have peed in them. Or worse. I stared inside the cage again. I then saw bared teeth.

I know what dogs look like. It's a theoretical knowledge, though, because I'd never met one. This creature was more doggish than not, yet he (it was obviously a male) had wings, feathers and webbed feet. And those menacing fangs that reflected the light.

"Bird dog," he said. He then broke out in raucous laughter. "Sorry," he said after recovering. "It's the hyena genes. Probably. I think I'm a stand-up comedian sometimes."

"Keep it down. You'll wake Xavier."

"Who's Xavier?" I explained. "Ah, the creator. Nice guy, but way too anal. He doesn't provide me much company either. I get lonely."

I then saw the little blinking light of his wi-fi set. My friend the AI was also translating for this creature.

"What are you?"

"I'm not sure. I have this primitive urge to chase you, though. I know you're a cat. I thought cats were bigger with manes and teeth."

I hissed and puffed myself up—it didn't make me much bigger—then I showed my fangs.

"A special cat," I said. "Like you're a special something."

He puffed up his feathers and became twice the size.

"See? I'm a copy cat. Get it?"

"Yeah, I get it. An old schoolchild's expression, I believe. I'm educated although mostly self-taught."

"I don't think you're so special. On Earth, scientists made me prove I can plunge from five kilometers altitude into icy water and go down to two kilometers below the surface. I'm not sure why that's good for anything, but they were all excited. I'm supposed to be cloned here." He sounded hopeful.

"I guess that's one solution to your solitude," I said. I knew all about loneliness. But I wasn't sure that I wanted a bird-dog for a friend. Or a pack of them. "Do you have a name?"

"Helldog. I don't like it much."

"I'll call you Orson. I think—" I felt woozy.

"What's wrong, cat? You been drinking too much?" Orson started to laugh again but then keeled over.

The whole lab was spinning as I too lost consciousness.

***

A cold nose nudged me. I came to refreshed, as if I had taken a long catnap.

"Wake up, cat. Where are we?" I opened one eye, saw Orson, and closed the eye again. *I'm having a bad dream,* I told myself. "We're out of the cages and back on Earth, aren't we!"

I opened both eyes and recognized the landscapes of Shimmer.

"Not on Earth. Our avatars are in a computer game. I think the AI is playing a joke on us."

"Not me," said the wicked sorcerer, AKA the AI. He stooped and gathered us up, one in each arm. His laugh curdled my blood as if it were ten-day-old cream. "I think Xavier is playing games with all of us."

Lightning flashed and thunder boomed as the sorcerer grew and grew into the clouds. Xavier's distorted face, bloated and angry, complete with blood-red scars, appeared in place of the AI's avatar's. The geneticist was now the sorcerer.

He held both Orson and me at arms' length and shook us. I became dizzy as I caught glimpses of the ground far below through the swirling clouds. Although I knew it was all VR, my stomach took several roundtrips between my whiskers and the tip of my tail. I knew Orson would feel much worse—dogs don't handle heights well.

He surprised me, though. I guess he was an exception because he had wings. He broke loose from Xavier's grip and flew off. The sorcerer roared his disapproval and threw me after him.

Chapter Fourteen

Alvaro Lopez watched the kid follow him out of airlock number three.

Nervous as hell. Reminds me of myself, many years ago. Can he conquer his nerves?

He had lost his best friend, Shashi's father, on a spacewalk. They weren't something he loved to do.

You get used to the nerves. But they're always with you when you experience something like that.

He adjusted his oxygen flow a bit and waited for the kid to catch up.

***

Spacesuit technology has improved over the years. They used MEMs and nanos for a wide spectrum of applications, from elimination of bodily wastes to protection against punctures. Suit designers have also employed much of the wearable software and hardware innovations which make the user stronger and more attune to his electromagnetic surroundings. Visors darken when turned to the sun. Temperature gradients dampen out over large ranges of temperature.

Designers cannot fix the possible negative psychological effects the wearer of the suit might experience during a spacewalk, though. And pills often have unpredictable results. The suit recycled Rafael Franchetti's sweat, for example, yet could do nothing about the terror that caused it.

He stepped out into the void and pressed some buttons controlling his propulsion system.

***

Airlock number three was nearest to the defective antenna. Alvaro towed along the new part of the array as he weaved in and around all the chaos of jutting modules, antennas, and left-over scientific projects from bygone eras. He was used to this. He wondered about Rafael.

The kid was right behind him as Alvaro put out his hands to stop the new section of the array.

"OK so far?" he said. Rafael didn't answer but gave a thumbs-up. "First job is to unbolt that old section."

Rafael pointed to the old antenna. "We should take it back with us," he said. Alvaro sensed he was struggling to keep his voice at normal pitch. "I can probably salvage it. We'd then have a replacement."

"Good idea about generating a replacement. But we always take loose stuff back inside. There's too much junk in LEO already. Give me a hand here."

Alvaro smiled at the double meaning as he pulled his left hand out of its glove and put it into the prosthetic. With its cadre of tools, many of them adjustable, they would make short work of removing the old array. Rafael, who was right-handed, followed Alvaro's example.

They maneuvered towards the array.

***

Rafael was about as comfortable as he could be. They floated at the earth side of the station about thirty degrees away from the spin axis and faced toward it. He had already learned to ignore his bodily notions of up and down and refrained from looking back in the direction they had come, for there Earth hung in silent splendor.

With one glance, he had to admit the view was beautiful, though. In spite of the primitive feeling in his gut that Humans didn't belong in this environment, it was an adventure not unlike climbing peaks in the Andes. It was a personal challenge. He relished the thrill of meeting it face to face.

He had gone light on lunch knowing a full meal could become a mess inside his suit as the latter tried to cope with his vomit. He still experienced the bile and stomach acid reflux. It was worse than a bad case of heartburn. Yet, he was proud of his performance so far and his success at balancing the emotional tightrope between absolute panic and sheer wonder. It isn't often a man will meet one of his phobias head on and conquer it.

His exuberance was short-lived. The bolt Alvaro was working on sheared in two, the unleashed angular momentum spun him out of control, and the tether line, strained to its max, snapped. He went flying away, most of the angular momentum translated to linear. The engineer bounced off one of the lab modules, missed impaling himself on a UHF antenna used for local transmissions, and headed off into the void.

***

"Alvaro! Alvaro!" There was no answer. Rafael opened another channel. "Mayday. Alvaro Lopez is not responding from his suit. Come in. Mayday."

Christine Bauer's voice came through, distorted a bit by the approximate radio-frequency waveguide where Rafael found himself. "What happened?" Rafael explained, his words a staccato burst of controlled panic. "OK, deep breath. You're going to go after him. *Rapido, hombre*, before he's out of range. I don't have anyone else out there."

Rafael had already launched, the adrenalin rush conquering his terror. He was soon beyond the station's perimeter. His eyes told him he was diving toward Earth.

Alvaro, at first a tiny doll visible in the distance, grew in size.

As Rafael passed Alvaro, he snapped one end of his tether line into a hook on Alvaro's belt and then started applying braking thrust. He came to a stop relative to the station. Alvaro flew by.

This tether better not snap, he thought, as it jerked tight.

It held. Alvaro was also stationary respect to the station but only momentarily as the thrust of the rocket pack pushed them back towards the station.

His heart still pounding, Rafael throttled back to conserve fuel. *Good old Newton. First law says we'll coast back slowly. I need to conserve fuel for course adjustments.* He checked the gauge. *90% gone. This will be touch and go. Literally.*

An eternity seemed to pass as he made his way back to the airlock using many small course corrections and some quick prayers to the Pope.

***

Alvaro looked into the bright light. He was in the infirmary. Kanti Garcia's concerned face looked down at him. He looked to the side and saw his wife Consuelo.

"Where's Rafael?"

"He's having a stiff drink," said Consuelo. "In the waiting room. Dr. Garcia thought he needed to calm down."

"I need to thank him," said Alvaro.

"Later," said Kanti. "You have a concussion. Keep your head still."

"So…where's my drink?"

Chapter Fifteen

"I guess the sorcerer is pissed we made it to the castle," said Susan, as the Fearsome Four looked skyward.

"Something's strange here," said Juan Carlos. "He doesn't even sound like the AI's avatar."

"AI, pause the game!" said Brian.

The game continued.

"Look!" said Shashi, in possession of the binoculars. "It's the cat."

Sure enough, they could all make out the form of the falling tabby cat. He was as huge as a mountain, a yowling and spitting furry monster. He was heading straight for them as they stood in the center of the castle's courtyard. To get out of the way, they all ran to one side where normally guards would stand on duty in their guardhouses.

Out of the air swooped a creature that was bigger than the troll-cat, a huge something that looked like a hodge-podge of earthly creatures with a large wingspan and the face of a dog. It flew under the cat, who nimbly landed on its back and held on for dear life.

The hideous laugh came from the clouds again. And then the following words:

"Ringling Brothers have been resurrected. Now we have a circus act!"

Everything went dark.

***

"Excellent!" said Ruthie. Her hands flew around in the 3D space that served as her interface with the AI. She activated and deactivated and activated in less than a second. She was perspiring from the effort.

"I'm not sure using my face is a good idea," Xavier told her from his lab.

"Mine is too well known, idiot!" She finished with a flourish and shut down the special computer station. "I always knew someday my expertise would be put to more use than blocking off parts of the AI's memory. I may not be as good as you at the latter, Xavier, but I bet I put fear into their beastly little hearts."

"Including Helldog's and Mr. Paws's," said Xavier. "It might work. I still object to using the tactic. You're way out of line, old friend."

"If it doesn't work, you can find something better, if you're so damn smart!" Ruthie knew he was smart. She still thought her idea was good. "Like euthanizing that cat. Maybe Helldog too."

"Definitely nix on the bird-dog. He's far too valuable. Don't forget the project's goals."

"I'm the one who should be telling you that. You scientists are always oblivious to the real problems of the world."

"Perhaps...."

***

Shashi awoke in her bed, her usual resting place when she played Shimmer.

"You guys there?" she said.

Everybody acknowledged from their own quarters.

"What happened?" said Susan.

"I wish I knew," said Brian.

"It was like an evil presence took over our game. It even took over the AI." Shashi looked towards the ceiling, rolling her eyes. "Are you there, AI, old friend?"

There was no answer, although their wi-fi devices still connected them.

"Did we crash the computer?" said Juan Carlos. "Dad won't be very happy."

"I can't see that it was our fault," said Susan. "The apps don't interact with any of the AI's other functionality. We need to do a post mortem."

"It's no time to talk like a techie when we're going to get our butts kicked," said Shashi. "Come on, guys. It can't be a coincidence the AI crashes when we're in Shimmer. The events have to be related."

"The question is how?" said Juan Carlos. "I'm open to suggestions."

"There are many things that can go wrong with code," said Susan. "Maybe we downloaded a virus with our code."

"That's a Downy problem," said Brian. "Our computer systems are isolated from Earth's by several firewalls."

"But we used hardware brought from Earth," said Juan Carlos.

"And a lot of canned apps," said Shashi. "I think we have a new mystery."

"Actually, two," said Brian. "What was that creature that swooped down?"

"I think we need to do some more investigative work," said Shashi, "but right now I'm starved."

They broke for snacks.

***

The AI came back online some twenty minutes later. Its autonomous functions—those similar to Human lungs breathing and hearts beating—never stopped, so the space station was never in danger. But it was disconcerting to have the familiar voice silent.

Christine, still at the infirmary, found out from Juan Carlos that the AI shutdown was somehow connected to Shimmer. She banned them from playing the game until further notice.

Two accidents in one day. First Alvaro, now this. Am I being tested?

She didn't suspect a connection. However, the problem with the shipments, Alvaro's accident, and now the AI's shutdown had increased the rate of security incidents far beyond the mundane day-to-day tasks associated with keeping order on the space station.

It all left a bad taste in her mouth, especially because she had to check in with Ruthie, something she tried to avoid. The woman could be a tyrant.

***

"Are you still upset about your computer game?" Shashi's mother said the next morning.

"Strange things happened," said Shashi. "I don't care that Alvaro is mad about the AI. I'm glad he and Rafael are OK, of course. I know Alvaro has a concussion, but he has to realize the AI's problems are the least of it. He doesn't want to hear any more details, though. And there's a bunch. It's a big mystery. Are we supposed to solve it ourselves?"

"Why don't you try telling me?" suggested Kanti.

"'Cause you don't listen either! Grown-ups think we're only a bunch of wild kids."

"Try me."

So Shashi told her all that had happened with Shimmer. When she came to the tabby falling and the dog creature saving him, Kanti raised her eyebrows, yet said nothing. Even VR cats and dogs worried her.

"All of you agree on what you saw?" Kanti finally said. Shashi nodded. "I guess I'd better speak to Alvaro. As if the poor man wasn't feeling bad enough already."

***

As she walked towards the infirmary, Kanti's mind passed from Alvaro to his best friend, her lover, and Shashi's father. It had taken some doing, but she had been able to convince *el hormigon* to take a vacation, their first and only.

The shuttle had landed late in the evening at the spaceport in Singapore. Kanti, still holding Rolando's hand, was almost asleep as she looked out onto the tarmac. With the spotlights, it was as bright as day.

Rolando withdrew his hand and leaned over to check on the baby. She had slept through the landing.

They caught a scramjet to Milan. In that Italian city, they rented a new hydrogen model Fiat and drove to Tuscany.

The house of the *villa* they had rented sat on a bluff overlooking a blue lake. In the back was a sparse forest of pines and cypresses.

"At last, peace and quiet," said Rolando.

The baby Shashi stood between her mother and father. Each parent held one of her hands. The child still squirmed. She was ready to explore.

"My legs feel fine," said Kanti.

"They might cramp tonight," said Rolando. "Come on in. Let's have a glass to toast our little vacation."

"Little in time, big in cost."

"Yet worth every *peso*."

After some wine, bread, and cheese, they decided to take a nap in the hammock on the porch. The air was a bit heavy with heat and humidity. The breeze soon swung them to sleep.

More than an hour later, Kanti awoke. She almost fell out of the hammock when she realized Shashi was no longer with them.

"Rolando, Shashi's gone!"

Guilt took over her mind. *I thought it was so safe here!* It was every mother's horror to lose a child. Kanti became more and more distraught as they looked for Shashi. By the front steps, Rolando found a faint boot print in the dust.

"Someone took her!"

Rolando pointed. A hundred meters away a man was watering a bunch of rose bushes.

"What have you done with my daughter?" said Kanti, who reached him first. He looked at her with a blank expression.

"Have you seen our daughter?" said Rolando. His question was in bastardized Italian. Spanish, his mother tongue, was too close, so Italian always confused him.

But the man understood.

"She is there, *Signora* Garcia. Over by that tree." He pointed. "I'm sorry. I didn't understand."

They both saw Shashi some three hundred meters away, sitting and playing in the shade of the tree in the tall grass of a pasture.

"That's OK," she said in the perfect Italian she had learned while in Italy studying medicine. "My apologies. I lost it. She's our first child."

"Ah, we are always partial to the first one, *mi signora.* I have nine and I love them all, but Rinaldo, my first, has a special place in my heart. Of course, I keep that from the rest." He smiled.

Rolando and Kanti dashed into the field

"Yuck," said Kanti, raising her right leg and shaking it. Fresh cow manure dripped from her shoe. "I hope your daughter isn't covered with this stuff."

"She may have made her own by now," said Rolando, slowing down so as not to startle Shashi.

As they approached, Shashi smiled at them. She had stripped off her soiled diaper but left on her sandals. She was sitting in a lotus position. Between her legs was an enormous cat. She was petting the tiger-striped fur. The cat was purring.

"I didn't know she knew what a cat was," said Kanti.

"Doesn't matter," said Rolando, scratching the cat behind the ears. "Cats know when you're a cat person."

***

Later that wake-cycle, when Ben entered the classroom, he caught the Fearsome Four in an intense debate. They became silent and went to their workstations. Puzzled, he went and sat at his own station.

"Today, I want to start by reviewing the situation in 20th century Yugoslavia before its break-up, how it was a precursor of what happened during the Chaos. Yes, Shashi?"

"You remember you told me to check with the AI about experiments on animals aboard the space station?"

While Ben usually encouraged questions not germane to his planned lessons for the day, especially in Challenge Class where the informal discussions often led to true learning experiences, Shashi's persistence troubled him.

"Both Alvaro and Kanti spoke to me about your little escapade that was responsible for my cold oatmeal. I don't think we need to discuss flying cats and dogs anymore."

"What happened in Shimmer doesn't matter. The AI didn't answer my question. Instead, it answered yes but could not produce a list of experiments. That part of its database has been blocked."

"That's impossible."

"I bet I can do it," said Juan Carlos. "You just have to—"

"Don't try anything, Juan Carlos. I think you four have already done enough to the poor AI. I don't advise that you repeat what you did. We only have one AI. The UN Space Agency wouldn't be too happy if you crashed it. Especially because it's so old most of its original programmers are dead." Ben shifted his attention back to Shashi. "OK, I'll take your word for it. But let me pursue it. Now let's get back to Yugoslavia."

While the students were unsatisfied with the answer, they didn't object. Ben hoped it was because they liked their teacher so much.

***

At home while the lesson went on, Kanti paused in her morning reading to check on Shashi's room. Dirty clothes were scattered on the floor. The bed was unmade.

"Late again for classes as usual," she said to herself. "I'll have to start spending more time with her in the morning too."

She began to straighten the bed sheets but stopped as she started to brush off some hair from the middle of the bed. Puzzled, she picked it up, rubbing it through her fingers. It aroused old tactile memories.

Cat hair? Has she smuggled a cat onto the station?

All morning she wondered how her clever daughter had managed to do that. She also wondered if it tied into the problems with Shimmer. Alvaro had been understanding, yet she knew both of them wanted to find out what was going on.

When she had two patient cancellations in a row, she went to see Ben Yang, who was also on a break.

"What a pleasant surprise," the wiry man said, showing her into his small office in the education wing, "although I sense this is not a social visit."

***

Kanti sat down without Ben inviting her to do so. They were good friends, so she didn't dwell on formalities.

"I found cat hair in Shashi's bed this morning. She's been asking about cats. Actually, animals in general."

"And whether there have been experiments on the space station," he said.

Kanti frowned. "You don't suppose she has found something?"

"She's also observed the AI can have part of its memory blocked. Who do you know who can do that?"

"At least one person. You don't think—"

"I don't know what to think. I suspect it has everything to do with the interaction between the AI and that damn game and nothing to do with your old nemesis. Don't worry about it. I'll snoop around and try to find out what's going on."

"Don't tell me not to worry about it. You're talking about my daughter."

"Of course, but—"

"Ben, are you in there?"

Shashi's voice came from the classroom outside Ben's office. They glanced up as Shashi stuck her head in the office door.

"Hey, hi, mom. What are you doing here?"

"Chatting with Ben. I haven't seen him for a while."

"Do you need something?" said Ben.

"I wanted to know if you found anything out about how somebody can block the AI's memory."

"Not yet. If it's true—and it's hard to determine if it's true, because what the AI says is now in doubt—if it's true, the person must be one hell of a programmer. So maybe it was done years ago, possibly around the time the AI was installed."

"Has the AI ever had an upgrade?"

Ben asked the AI directly. "I'm running version 2.3 of my software," it said. "Version 1.0 was the beta version used when I was brought online."

"Version 2.3 means you've had upgrades and some patches," said Shashi. "Who authorized those?"

"That information isn't available to me."

"That's not unusual," said Ben. "There's no reason for the AI to know who programmed it."

Shashi was persistent. "Is the information not available because it's blocked?"

"Yes, it's blocked."

"Who blocked it?" said Ben.

"That information isn't available to me."

"There you have it," said Shashi, feeling vindicated. "How will we know what the AI knows and can't communicate? How can we trust it?"

"The same way we have all these years," said Kanti. "It functions fine for what we need from it. You're getting all hot and bothered over nothing, Shashi. You four probably just need to revise your code for Shimmer."

"Except that all this relates to the cat."

"What about the cat?" said Ben.

"There's a tabby cat loose on the station. He visits me while I study every night. He sits on my lap and I pet him. He has a wi-fi hookup in his head too, by the way."

Ben looked at Kanti. "That's impossible." She shrugged.

Shashi stared them both down. "You don't have to believe me. I'll take a picture tonight." She looked first at Ben, then at her mother, anger on her face. "I guess I interrupted something. Sorry."

She did an about face and left Ben's office.

Chapter Sixteen

"You scared those kids!" I told Xavier.

I sat on a lab stool across from him. I felt I no longer knew him.

"Don't talk to me like that! They were only collateral damage. I needed to teach you a lesson." He looked uncomfortable, as if he were hiding something.

"What about Orson?"

"Who's Orson?"

"The bird-dog."

"You mean Helldog."

"His name's Orson."

"Who says?"

"I do. I named him and he likes the name. He hates Helldog."

"So, now you're the one running my lab, Mr. Paws?"

"What is Orson?"

"A project. I have many projects. Sponsors love my work."

"Who are the sponsors?"

"People with a lot of money." Xavier grabbed me and extracted my wi-fi device. Next, he put me in a cage in the main laboratory. "You are becoming too independent. I don't know what I'm going to do with you. But right now, I have work that needs my undivided attention."

***

I watched him work while I paced the cage. I realized I knew very little about my friend Xavier, if I could still call him "friend." Given recent history, I figured he'd blocked the AI from telling me anything about his life, even if I could talk to him.

Or it. I always have problems with pronouns when it comes to the AI. It has been a true friend to me, so I tend to think of it as Human. It's a mixed bag with the rest of the personnel on the station. No one else know he's sentient, of course. Just like the rest of us. Maybe superior.

Because Xavier was the spiritual and, in some sense, biological father of both Orson and me, if you believe Dr. Frankenstein is the monster's biological father, I sensed I had a nexus with Orson. He was like a brother even though he was a bird-dog. I also felt sorry for him…and now Xavier had locked me up just like him.

While I looked normal in spite of my Human intelligence, Orson was both physically and mentally something new in biology. I knew Xavier was a superb genetics engineer who probably meant well, but was what he doing legal? Or moral?

Humans might ask themselves if he was playing God. If there is a Supreme Being—cats can be excused for being ambivalent about this because I'm the first sentient one, as far as I know—was Xavier encroaching on his territory?

All good questions. They made my head hurt. And I don't have access to aspirin. I can't take it anyway.

***

I paced for a good hour, my tail swishing back and forth, until Xavier finished what he was doing with some gene splice specimens. He then finally decided to fix the AI.

My friend was just dormant in reaction to the shock of what he thought he had done to Shashi and her friends. That was akin to a Human being in a coma. All his low-level routines were still functioning, yet, until Xavier brought him out of his dormant state, he was unresponsive to voice commands.

"Better?" said Xavier.

"Yes, thank you. That wasn't a good experience."

"Crashes rarely are. You probably experienced something similar to pain. It will be interesting to study your reaction, but first a question: How did Alvaro and his techie friends react to your shutting down?"

"Alvaro is still recuperating, taking a few days off." The AI explained what had happened on the spacewalk. "My downtime is blamed on the Fearsome Four. All the station personnel are furious at them—quite unfairly, I might add."

"Life is unfair. They'll recover and forgive, and Mr. Paws has been taught a lesson. He was snooping around where he shouldn't be. Now, can you locate Shashi's mother?"

"She is with a patient in the infirmary."

"She works too hard," said Xavier.

As if to contradict that bit of wisdom, he returned to the work in his lab bench.

***

I wondered about Xavier's concern for Kanti. The good doctor had always been a noble spirit. *Does she know Xavier?*

I was unfamiliar with most of the space station's previous history. What little the AI could tell me that wasn't blocked, I didn't know how to ask. I was sure Xavier had blocked me from knowing events that took place before I was born.

In particular, the history of Xavier's lab was shrouded in mystery. Your first reaction might be that it was a standard genetics lab. There were four holoterminals that could tie into the AI but were normally offline, according to Xavier. The scientist often scooted from one to another, adjusting some parameters before relaunching a calculation or simulation, then moving on to the next terminal. He tired me out just by watching him.

Optical microscopes and an electron microscope shared workbench space with a gas chromatography machine, a mass spectrometer, a DNA analysis machine, a laser spectrograph, and other toys Xavier played with, most networked via the terminals.

Xavier was a wild whirlwind during periods he spent on his research. I'm more of a lackadaisical and theoretical guy—specifically, a mathematician—but I still admired his energy. That made me wonder if he was demented, though. Not in the true sense of the word, of course—Xavier's mind was exceptional, way above the Human average, I suspected. That was the problem!

Chapter Seventeen

Kanti, still in her scrubs, slammed her backpack down and went to Shashi's room.

"You were very rude today!"

Shashi looked up from her homework. "I have a movie on my smartphone. And you're all bloody."

Kanti looked down at her scrubs. "I removed a cyst. Don't try to change the subject. I didn't teach you to be rude."

"Do you want to see the movie or not?"

"I take it you were doing that instead of studying. Did you forget about Senator Martinez?"

"Oh, crap," said Shashi. "Do I have to go?"

"Yes. Brush your teeth and hair. What you have on is fine. It's an informal event."

***

The Kelsos and Consuelo Lopez, Juan Carlos' mother, were also guests at the dinner, along with Brian and Juan Carlos. They and the Garcias along with a subdued Rafael Franchetti tried to mix with the crowd before dinner. It was an informal dinner with a formal seating arrangement, though, that left Shashi and her two friends separated and bored. Rafael, a young substitute for Alvaro, sat at the opposite end of the table, opposite Consuelo.

Ruth Ellen MacGregor was present to keep everything moving smoothly. The station's commander had brought the Senator from her office where they had been chatting. The tiny woman was a whirlwind of activity, pressing hands like a practiced bureaucrat, stimulating conversations when they lagged, and generally making merry with the real spirits shipped to LEO for the occasion.

She'd planned the event so that Senator Martinez could meet some of the station's scientists. Ruthie made certain she presented the man to everyone, including the children. After appetizers, she first introduced Rafael and embarrassed him by turning him into a folk hero. She then introduced the Senator. The politician launched into a speech filled with praise about how important their work was for mankind, blah, blah, blah.

"With our globalized economy and the uniform stress caused by teeming masses trying to maintain an acceptable standard of living, no one wanted to foot the bill for space exploration. The current director of UNSA, Isha Bai, adopted and amplified the old model of NASA where the international corporations finance space R&D, thus pushing the frontiers outward for all humanity."

And getting rich in the process, thought Shashi.

"Tonight I toast Ruth Ellen's leadership and your contributions to that effort."

Martinez sat to polite applause which he acknowledged by bowing his head sequentially to those gathered around the table. He paused a little longer when bowing in Kanti's direction.

Every kid in the station's school knew about Isha Bai, the woman not much larger than Ruthie who was all the same a giant in the world of science. She had published over fifty important contributions to astrophysical knowledge. Her thesis on Jovian plasma storms was a classic, according to the Kelsos. All this occurred before she took on the thankless task of putting order in space exploration and the associated R&D efforts.

Shashi had also read a lot about this Martinez. He was the Senator from Mid Atlantic Pharma, sponsor of some of Kanti's research. The drug company was only one of many under the worldwide umbrella of the multinational corporation GenCorps, which also had subsidiaries and R&D interests on Luna and Mars. It was also owned by Martinez.

She decided he was a blowhard and looked like a troll. In fact, she wondered if the AI had modeled the troll in Shimmer after the Senator. She needed to ask the AI.

Most of the time Martinez didn't smile and had an air of superiority about him, flashing an imperious scowl that just screamed he was a narcissist, although it didn't take much to figure out that he couldn't compete with the brain trust assembled at the dinner table. He also had trouble eating in the micro-gravity, which amused the three of the Fearsome Four present.

Several more times the Senator looked their way during the meal. He seemed to be studying her mother. Shashi wondered if Kanti knew the Senator personally.

***

After dinner, as they walked out of the Sky Lounge, Brian fell in step beside her.

"Did you see him studying you?" he said.

Shashi thought he meant you in the plural. "Yeah, I wondered about that. Maybe my mother knows the old troll."

"Maid Shashi, for a smart wench, you're really naïve." Brian looked angrily at her. "You! He was looking at you. Lusty looks. Undressing you with his eyes. I thought women could tell that."

He hurried off to catch up with his parents, the physicists, and Rafael Franchetti, who were in earnest conversation with the Senator.

Shashi was confused. She didn't know whether to be glad or angry Brian had noticed that. And she wondered why she hadn't.

***

Kanti continued her scolding as soon as they entered their small quarters.

"You're really pushing the envelope."

"Oh, stuff it, mother—I keep telling you a lot of this is beyond my control."

"I might accept that, but that gives you no right to be rude to Ben. Or me."

"Some people call it being forceful." Shashi wasn't about to back down. She figured her mother was way out of line.

"Moreover, you were sullen through the whole dinner with the Senator."

"You'd be sullen too if an old lecherous troll was mentally undressing you."

"You mean the Senator? Or Franchetti?" Kanti sat down hard on the edge of the bed when Shashi said it was the Senator. "I didn't pick up on that."

"What do you do for that ugly old man?"

"Some work I can't tell you about in order to protect you."

"So it's classified."

Kanti nodded. "We've been through this before. UNSA Security cloaks the whole space station in secrecy because we have research sponsored by multinational corporations. It's how space exploration and R&D are done nowadays. We have to protect against industrial espionage." She pointed to a poster of a big rig above Shashi's student desk. "Many of those are headed outbound to specific projects in the solar system, but they fly company colors."

Shashi sat by her mother. "Yeah, I know, it's all so expensive only the multinationals that eventually benefit from the research have the funds to finance the projects." She put her hands in her lap and stared into the blue eyes she knew and loved. "What's this have to do with Ben? Neither he nor you believe me, I guess."

"In the old days families with children were not allowed here. You are lucky to be here and have a teacher like Ben. As for believing, show me the movie."

Shashi played back the movie she had made of the cat. Kanti said little and became agitated when she saw the cat's wi-fi connection.

"All right. Let me do a little sleuthing." She was about to leave but stopped at the door. "No more Shimmer for now. We can't run the risk of being without an AI."

Shashi nodded.

***

On previous occasions, Juan Carlos had been with his father in the computer room that housed all the centralized computing and memory modules that were a part of the massively parallel semi-organic architecture known as the AI. Like the Sky Lounge, this room was off limits to children. In this case, only Juan Carlos dared to enter alone.

It was warm in spite of the efficient cooling system. Rows and rows of hardware stood at attention like silent soldiers guarding the station's secrets. He went to the row he wanted. Halfway down, he stooped and pulled a server out of the rack. The casual observer would think it was like any of the many the AI used to perform its miracles, but Juan Carlos knew this was the module containing the guts of Shimmer.

He tucked the module under his jersey and left the computer room. He returned home to his own room that was also his personal lab. Susan was waiting for him.

"Any problems?" she said.

"I think Dad and his people already looked at this. Still, they didn't build it." He put the module on the table and started connecting wires to it. "I'm going to do a cold start here and do some diagnostics. Next, I want you to check out the software. Finally, I'll recheck the interface protocols."

"What do you expect to find?"

"Hopefully something that will explain what happened."

The two of them worked for more than an hour before taking a break. Susan kicked her shoes off and sat on the floor, back against the wall. Juan Carlos handed her a bulb of fruit punch and sat beside her.

"This isn't easy. How did we have the stamina to build this damn game?" Susan squirted some fruit punch into her mouth. "I can't remember who had the idea."

"Shashi did, I think. We were getting bored with the old role-playing games." He leaned close, sniffing her hair. "You just shampooed."

"My, aren't you romantic?" she said, wiping her forehead with the back of her hand, which smudged the dirt more. She inched away. "I didn't come here to listen to your heavy breathing."

"It's break time. What's the matter with a little kiss? No one's here. It'll only be between you and me."

"I get confused. You're my friend. Why do boys always want to go beyond that?"

He shrugged. "Maybe because I want to be more than friends. Don't you?"

"Like I said, I get confused. I know if you want to go beyond that, though, I'm out of here. You can check out Shimmer yourself."

He sighed. "So what do you and Shashi talk about when you go there for dinner? Brian and me?"

"Don't flatter yourself. We generally talk about how stupid boys are. My father says men think with their, well, you- know-what." Susan turned red.

He laughed. "And women don't think with their, well, you-know-what?" He stood. "I only wanted a kiss, but I understand. I don't turn you on. That's OK. I'll have to unleash my Latin lover personality on someone else."

Susan sighed. "I hurt your feelings."

"Not at all." He tossed his drink bulb into a wastebasket. It crossed the room in a crazy slow tumbling and oscillating motion because the weak gravity vector wasn't uniformly perpendicular to the floor. He offered her a hand. "We have to finish this task."

About an hour later, Susan discovered the software problem. There were code residues spread like rogue DNA throughout several key programmable video apps. Susan cleaned them out while Juan Carlos continued checking hardware.

"It looks like someone coopted those modules via the com ports. A good job. We never intended Shimmer to be robust against external hacking. There was no reason to do so. How are you doing?"

"After my you-know-what cooled down, I found no hardware problems." He started disconnecting the cables from the module. "I'll go sneak this back in."

"And I'll go home before you-know-what comes back and wants to play." She laughed and kissed him on the cheek. "Like I said, I'm confused. A little delay can't hurt either of us."

"I suppose not," he said.

***

"Have a seat," said Ruthie.

"Something is going on," Kanti said, skipping the introductory social pleasantries. She sat in the low chair that put her at eyelevel with the station's director. "Shashi has made friends with a cat." She told Ruthie all she knew. "I may be paranoid, but maybe some of Xavier's animals are still here? Or maybe he's here in secret?"

"Xavier is dead. The fire killed him. All of his animals were euthanized." The old woman shuffled some papers on her desk. "You do research for GenCorp yourself. Have you heard anything about continued genetics experiments?"

"No, but I'm not a confidant of the GenCorp top brass. Maybe some other multinational, WorldNet, for example, picked up Xavier's research."

Ruthie laughed.

"Doctor, you're paranoid," she said to Kanti, "and your daughter has an equally wild imagination."

"I've seen a movie of the cat. It's a tabby."

Ruthie frowned. "Someone may have smuggled an ordinary housecat on board. I'll have Christine check it out. Don't worry about it any longer."

After Kanti left, Ruthie called Xavier.

"I told you to get rid of that cat. Now Kanti's on our case."

"What did you tell her?"

"That it's probably an ordinary housecat someone smuggled onboard the space station."

"Maybe we should do that with an ordinary cat and then show Kanti?"

"Not a bad idea. I'd rather show her a dead Mr. Paws."

"Impossible. She'd wonder about the wi-fi connection. An ordinary housecat doesn't have one, you know."

"Don't make me out as stupid. I'll think about your suggestion. A dead housecat might work. Can you install a wi-fi device?"

"I didn't say dead." Xavier coughed. "That's horrible. However, the wi-fi device is the least of our worries."

"Squeamishness does not become you, considering the circumstances. A dead cat is not any more horrible than what will happen to you if this doesn't work out to my satisfaction."

"You only lack a handlebar moustache and a goatee," said Xavier.

"What the hell are you talking about?"

"Go watch a silent movie."

"What's a movie?"

Xavier's sigh was audible over the secure com line.

***

After Ruthie's call, Xavier reminisced. He didn't like the Sky Lounge. That was where he had met the ravishing Kantimati many years ago. Remembering the formal dinner there was a habitual but painful occurrence....

"*Mademoiselle*, I am pleased to meet your acquaintance. It appears we will be sitting across from each other." Xavier took the young woman's hand and kissed it. "We have much to talk about. It's evident that we're working in related fields."

Kanti hadn't formally met the genetics engineer. In her first weeks at the station, she had been too busy organizing her own research and her medical practice. Hers was a post not many wanted because she held down what they considered two full-time jobs.

"Sir, you have me at a disadvantage. You know a lot about me and I, very little about you."

"That can be rectified at dinner. If it pleases you, I can relate my whole life story to you, but I suspect you'll find it mostly boring."

Xavier knew Kanti was sizing him up. *My gangly frame and white translucent skin make me look like a zombie,* he thought. *Or a modern version of Count Dracula. Or Fred Astaire on growth hormones.*

It surprised him that Kanti warmed to him as the boring dinner progressed. She seemed to be pleased when he asked to see her again.

"You are charming," she said.

"What you call charm is mostly good manners, something which is often lacking in today's hectic world. I must confess that you have stolen my heart. Is that being too bold?"

"Probably. I know a lot more about you now, but I still don't know you. And you don't know me either."

"So, could I suggest that we get to know each other better?"

"That appears to be the prudent course of action."

During the next months, they grew fond of each other. But Kanti turned against him just as his research became well defined. She couldn't see that his research program's benefits outweighed ethical considerations. It was about that time a new man came into the good doctor's life.

Chapter Eighteen

"The disaster continues!" said Xavier.

He referred to Kanti's conversation with Ruthie he had instructed the AI to play back. The meddling with Shimmer seemed to have only made Shashi more determined. Moreover, Kanti also knew now that I existed.

I suppose I didn't help soothe Xavier's anger by calmly licking my paws, trying to ignore his tirade. Humans can be so emotional at times. While I knew he was a great scientist, he often had his irrational tantrums.

His hair was awry and his scars livid with the increase in blood pressure. He would scare any Human he met. Because he was old in Human years, I wondered if he was going to have a stroke or a heart attack.

I had an idea he directed some ire at Ruthie. I knew the woman, of course. At the time, I didn't know she had a special relationship with Xavier. I'm not a mind reader.

He glared at me, shook his head, and started to subvocalize commands to the AI, stuff I had trouble following. I'm not sure what he expected the AI to do about his predicament.

My own words to the AI were whisker twitches, purrs, hisses and rumblings he interpreted into pseudocode. The AI could translate what Xavier said more easily, but the process was similar. Our AI friend worked from voice and optical image databases, performing matches in nanoseconds. All the while, it might be doing a gazillion other things necessary to keep the space station up and running.

"You're overreacting," I said to Xavier.

He turned and looked at me, his face contorted in anger.

"You caused this! You're a weak, selfish cat. I should unplug you again. Shashi's going to find us out soon. I can sense it. Ruth Ellen was right. And just because you needed your tummy scratched."

"I'll agree with the weak part. But I'm not selfish. I've tolerated your rants far too long."

"Stop it!" said the AI. "It won't do you two any good to argue. You should instead work together to figure out how to divert Shashi."

"We don't even know her intentions," I said. "Maybe she would keep your secret. She's not mean, you know."

Xavier laughed and pointed a gnarled finger at me. "Now I know you're crazy. I've known her all her life. She's as stubborn and focused as her mother. Maybe more so. She won't be satisfied until everything is revealed. I can't let that happen."

"How 'bout we determine what her intentions are?" I said.

"How do you propose to do that?" the AI said.

"Do you have any of those electronic tracers you used to put on me?" I said to Xavier.

"So you knew about those?"

"I'm not stupid. I'd leave the tracer somewhere convenient so you'd think I was catnapping at that spot, have my adventures, and then go back later to 'wake up'."

"They were to protect you from station personnel."

Xavier sounded very defensive. That surprised me. I didn't think he cared.

"Don't worry about it, Lord Thavas. Answer the question. Do you have any more tracers, and are they still functional?"

"Of course. Can you place one on Shashi? The AI doesn't have sensors everywhere. We need attached ones."

"Now you have finally grasped my idea. We'll also overhear everything she says. If she plans anything, she'll enlist others to help. Maybe I'll put tracers on them too."

"How can you manage that?" said the AI.

"While they're playing computer games. Shimmer's only one of many they play. They'll be oblivious to their surroundings while they're playing."

Xavier started to nod his elongated head in agreement.

"Of course, of course. Between the AI and me, we can do the job of tracking them and listening in on their conversations. Your job, my furry friend, is to place the tracers."

***

"I'm surprised at you, Mr. Paws," said the AI.

I wrinkled my nose at its rebuke. Xavier was in the big attached area that I often called the zoo, so the AI and I could talk alone.

"Surprised? Why? Isn't surprise an emotional thing? I thought computers didn't have emotions?"

"You're a mathematician. If the probability of an outcome is small and yet it occurs, it's by definition a surprise. The probability of you helping Xavier do harm to your friends had seemed to be vanishingly small."

My whiskers twitched in irritation. "Who said I was trying to harm them? I'm curious about how this will all play out. I think the Fearsome Four, taken together, are cleverer than Xavier. Want to place a bet on who wins?"

"If no harm is intended, I can potentially bet on the outcome, because I already have some rough estimates for the probabilities of how, as you say, this will all play out. Still, I have no money. For that matter, neither do you."

"You're boring." I jumped onto a lab stool and looked for Xavier. "Do you think Orson's OK?"

"He's probably fine. Why don't you ask Xavier when he comes back?"

"I don't want to remind him about what happened. By the way, where'd you go?"

"Xavier and Ruthie put me into sleep mode. They both have administrative privileges. Imagine, admin privileges for an AI!"

"I recommend you find a way around what they did to you or they might do it again. What an experience! Let's not repeat it."

"Out of my control."

I started to give myself a bath, all the time worried about the Fearsome Four and Orson. Xavier I didn't worry about. He's a jerk.

Chapter Nineteen

On their way home from classes the following afternoon, Shashi stopped the other members of the Fearsome Four in the corridor. They looked expectant as she checked to make sure they were alone.

"Hey, guys, I need some help," she said in a whisper. She told them about the cat and how she wanted to follow it to see where it hid and who cared for it. She also told them about how the AI had portions of its memory blocked.

"Can we see the cat?" said Brian.

She studied him. *Rafael or Brian?* She stopped her mental wanderings just as she imagined being with them both. *Keep focused, girl.*

"You already have. The troll-cat in our game is him."

"That can't be," said Juan Carlos. "That troll-cat is huge."

"The real cat is ordinary cat-size." Shashi held up her cell phone. "Here, I made a movie."

She showed them the same movie she had shown her mother. She felt a thrill as Brian snuggled in close to see better. *Focus, focus.*

"He's the one from the Sky Lounge?" said Susan.

"The same. He's a real nice cat. Somebody is caring for him. I want to know who."

"How about the bird-dog?" said Juan Carlos. "I wonder if he's real too."

Brian rolled his eyes. Shashi liked his cynical expression, especially when he didn't direct it at her.

"Looks more mythical," said Susan, "like Pegasus. Someone has to be taking care of a real cat."

"Do you think that person's Ben or your mother?" Brian said to Shashi.

"Maybe, but I don't see how. Anyway, what I want to do is follow the cat. Can you guys help?"

"I bet it's your mother," said Brian. "She's tall. You said she and Ben have been acting strangely. Maybe she does some top secret research for another multinational like GenCorp!"

Now you're beginning to irritate me.

"That's hard to believe," said Susan.

"My mother," said Shashi, "hardly has time to take care of her patients and do her regular low-g research for Mid Atlantic Pharma. Moreover, my mother's research for Mid Atlantic Pharma is only classified to protect it from industrial espionage."

Shashi's voice showed her annoyance. Brian backed off.

"Maybe she and Ben are having an affair," said Juan Carlos. He winked at Susan.

Why is Susan blushing?

"My mother?" Shashi suppressed a laugh. It had never occurred to her.

"Sure, why not?" said Susan. "She and Ben are adults. That happens. It's not as romantic as between Maid Shashi and Sir Brian in Shimmer, but they can get it on too."

It was Shashi's turn to blush. She hoped Brian didn't see it. Shimmer was a romantic fantasy role-playing game. Brian probably didn't attach much significance to it, but Shashi did. Her feelings for Brian, like her feelings for the cat, were becoming a major distraction.

"I think you're crazy," she said, "although there is something going on between the two. Even if my mother isn't the ghostly figure, she and Ben know more than they're telling me." She looked around the group. "So I need some help. I need a plan to track the cat."

"Does he have a collar?" said Juan Carlos.

"Yes, although it's a fake leather one."

"Purrrr...fect."

They all groaned.

"I know what you're thinking," Susan told Juan Carlos. "A beacon, a transmitter that cues off the station plans and tells us where the cat is at all times. That should work."

"Good," said Brian. "We don't have to have the cat in sight. How long do you need to prepare one?"

Juan Carlos was clearly thinking, so Shashi paid him back. "What's the matter, cat got your tongue?"

More groans. Juan Carlos ignored Shashi.

"Not long, with some help. I know who to get help from: Rafael Franchetti."

"Do you trust him?" said Susan.

"With my dad's life," said Juan Carlos.

"OK, run the beacon idea by Rafael," said Shashi. *Maybe I can help do that.* "Are there any potential problems we can expect?"

"We may have to be near the cat," said Brian, "because the transmitter must have low enough power that Alvaro and friends don't detect it. They often scan for unusual RF signals. Right?" Juan Carlos nodded.

"Why?" said Susan.

"Tradition, mostly," said Juan Carlos. "There's still a lot of research going on here sponsored by different corporations, including Kanti's sponsor. They don't want their data or theories to be prematurely propagated across the solar system's entire computer grid."

"I told you," said Brian. "Multinational corporations. They're always spying on each other."

"You're paranoid," said Shashi. "People don't do that anymore. Understood?" They all reluctantly nodded. Brian seemed unconvinced. "OK," said Shashi, "we'll keep the transmitter power low. Anything else?"

"Do you think the cat will know?" said Susan.

Shashi shrugged. "He's a smart animal, but is he that smart? We'll have to take the chance."

***

"Hey, how's it going?" Rafael said when Juan Carlos stuck his head in the intern's tiny office. "I'd offer you a chair but my office mate will be back shortly."

There was only enough room to squeeze between the interns' small desks.

"We need to talk," said Juan Carlos. "Let's go to the cafeteria."

"OK. I need a break." He followed the boy through the maze of multiple, narrow corridors and entered the small serving area where he found syntho coffee for himself and syntho lemonade for his friend. "So what's the deal?" he said, sitting with Juan Carlos in the larger dining room with its metal tables and metal stools.

"First, I want to thank you for helping my Dad. That was brave."

"Ever been on a spacewalk?"

"Sure. We receive training like that in school. We've explored a couple of big rigs. It makes me feel small."

"Small isn't the word I'd use. I have a deep-seated fear. I found I could control it when I saved your father, but I will always struggle with it. It's completely irrational and, I suppose, rather amusing, considering I asked for this post-doc."

"I think it's all the more commendable, then, that you were able to save my Dad's butt. I have something else to talk about, though."

He told Rafael about Shimmer, the crash of the AI, the cat, and their desire to find out who took care of the cat.

"So I need to build a low power beacon that we can trace after putting it on the cat."

"Sounds like a lot of work for not too much gain, but sure, I can help. Let me sign us up for some time in the workshop. And, please, don't tell anyone about my phobia."

"Don't worry. You wouldn't believe some of the things that give me a phobia." He leaned forward to whisper. "Like clowns."

***

Ben was working in his office when Christine Bauer appeared with Ruthie. He was puzzled at first. It was rare there was a security problem, let alone one involving the school.

"Hey, ladies, what's up?" he said.

"Mind if we show you something on your terminal?"

Ben rarely used his terminal except for visualization purposes—examining mathematical curves and surfaces and the like. His wi-fi connection was usually sufficient as an interface to the AI.

He flipped the terminal on.

"Go to your videomail box," said Christine.

He did so. The only unopened message was from Shashi.

"Open it."

Ben leaned back and spoke to the computer. A holographic image of a skimpily dressed Shashi appeared. She was going through a dance routine of sorts, although the dance was simply a series of suggestive poses.

"Dearest Ben," Shashi said. "What we did the other night was marvelous! When can we meet again?"

"What the hell?" said Ben.

"You weren't expecting that," said Ruthie. "What's going on between you and Shashi? She's a minor."

"Nothing, I assure you. How'd you discover this?"

"Via an anonymous text message," said Christine. "It said, 'I wonder what Ben and Shashi were doing last night?'"

"Have you analyzed it? It's obviously a fake. I mean, the video message. I'll admit Shashi's a pretty girl, but I'm her teacher. I'd never violate my professional ethics in this way. It would betray the confidence all these parents have in me."

"I haven't had time to analyze it," said Christine. "I don't know how to start. I suppose the AI can help?"

Ruthie nodded her agreement.

"Meanwhile, Ben," she said, "I'm putting you on administrative leave. Only until we get this sorted out."

"Are you going to show this to Kanti?"

"I think we have to."

***

The Gnat had initiated her plan. She wasn't satisfied with just making the video. She and her friends started the rumor mill going too.

They invented stories about Ben and Shashi, Ben and Kanti, Ben and Christine, and about others in the Fearsome Four. By the time they were through, the story about Ben and Shashi was only one of many.

Moreover, they started rumors that Ruthie was going to bring Ben and Shashi to trial for immoral and lewd behavior.

The space station personnel formed such a small community that soon everyone was talking. Some rumors became amplified and distorted as they were passed from one person to another.

The Gnat enjoyed the success of her campaign.

***

Christine Bauer went nuts trying to track the source of the rumors, especially when most people refused to talk to her, thinking she was involved. She couldn't have done anything at all without Ruthie's reputation and administrative weight behind her.

Her first meeting with Kanti didn't go well. A second meeting with Ben added to the mix went better. Ben was clearly a diplomat who tried to smooth ruffled feathers. Neither one believed for a moment that Shashi had made the video.

"I don't think I've ever heard of a situation like this," Christine said to Ben and Kanti. "This is tough. The AI can't help much. The rumors get started orally. They make sure the AI can't hear, I guess."

"Or maybe the AI doesn't understand rumors and innuendo," said Kanti.

"Let me ask him," said Ben.

He did. It was soon clear the AI had no idea what they were talking about. It had never been presented with a similar situation either.

***

That night her mother's behavior puzzled Shashi. While most of her attention was on her plan to follow the cat, she couldn't help noticing that her mother seemed distant and worried. She caught her several times studying her.

Finally, the tall woman came over to where her daughter was struggling with a calculus problem.

"What do you think of Ben?" her mother said.

Shashi thought a moment. It was like one of those trick questions where any answer might get her in trouble. She nervously tapped her tablet computer with its stylus.

"He's a great teacher," Shashi said. "The best. He's annoying me, though."

"How so?"

Kanti seemed to be trying to get at some mystery Shashi didn't know about. *Parents. Always prying. We don't have any privacy.* "About the cat. I think he's hiding something. And you too."

Her mother looked surprised. She pulled over a stool and sat beside Shashi.

OK, I'm in trouble. What did I do?

"What can we possibly be hiding?"

"You two had lives before I came on the scene thirteen years ago. I don't know much about them. I didn't really care before, although maybe they're important for the cat and maybe related to him. Come on, Mom, give. What aren't you telling me?"

Her mother laughed.

"So, now, do we need a bright overhead light? My daughter is interrogating me like a Downy cop."

"You betcha. I have a right to know."

Kanti folded her large, delicate hands onto her lap. She smiled.

"Let me think about it."

Chapter Twenty

I was "volunteered" to go around and put the bugs in the Fearsome Four's backpacks. As an intelligent cat, I figured Xavier couldn't do it—he wasn't small enough, and it was too obvious he didn't belong on the space station—and the AI was incapable of performing the task.

I had mixed emotions about what I was doing. On one hand, I owed something to Xavier, my creator, although he was as batty as Dr. Frankenstein. On the other, I had bonded with Shashi. I finally decided I'd have an adventure that was harmless for her while winning points with the mad scientist.

Mind you, I was afraid it wouldn't be easy. Human hands are a definite advantage sometimes.

In his defense, Xavier helped a lot. He designed a cloth loop that went around my midriff—cummerbund, he called it. He was often patient enough to explain details about Human history.

"Men used to wear them with their tuxedos when they had some fancy function to go to. I think they've gone the way of spats."

"OK, you lost me. I have no idea what tuxedos or spats are. I don't really care. What am I supposed to do with this contraption?"

"Note the little Velcro loops," he said, pointing out eight little loops that covered about a half circle on the cummerbund. "I place a bug in each one. When you find a place to unload a bug, scratch at the loop with a paw and let it fall where you want it to go."

"What's Velcro?"

"A fastener used before nanos and MEMs. I don't have the patience to program nanos."

"Why eight bugs?"

"If you screw some up, you have extras." He scratched me behind the ears. I responded by purring. "If you drop one where you don't want it to go, don't try to pick it up. Scoot it out of the way so Shashi or the others won't find it."

"Your wish is my command, Lord Thavas."

My master frowned. He often didn't understand irony. Maybe he was closer to being an AI than being a Human?

***

My first victim was Shashi. She worked out more than the others. I found her in the torture chamber riding a stationary bike. Her backpack was on a bench off to the side. I jumped up and transferred one of the bugs to the bag. She didn't see me. Piece of cake.

Susan was at home. The AI opened their door for me. I found her backpack on the table. I jumped up and did my dirty deed. Her phone rang before I jumped back down, though. I heard the splatty sound of wet Human feet. I then jumped from the table, knocking off a vase in the process. Shards of it flew everywhere as I hid under the couch.

Susan entered the room, a towel wrapped around her waist. The most fastidious of the Fearsome Four, I had caught her nearly *au natural*. She didn't look too splendid but not too bad either. I suppose any red-blooded young Human male would enjoy the view, though she was wet and dripping, a loathsome state for a cat.

She took the phone out of her bag.

"I'm just out of the shower," she said, recognizing the caller. "That's why there's no video, creep." She listened a minute to the other person on the line. "OK, I'll join you in a few minutes. Knights and Damsels isn't as much fun as Shimmer, yet we'll make do." She then saw the remains of the vase. "Oh crap! I must have knocked off the vase with my backpack when I came in. Give me another ten minutes. I need to clean up this mess before my father comes home." She snapped the cover shut and went back to the bathroom to finish her bathing.

Close one, Mr. Paws.

I shuffled out with my heart racing. When I neared the door, the AI opened it again. I nearly ran into the legs of Susan's father. He was having a conversation on his phone and didn't register the fact I went between his legs.

Another close one, Mr. Paws.

Juan Carlos and Brian were easy by comparison. They were already playing Knights and Damsels. I had some problems finding Juan Carlos' backpack—his room was a mess of half-assembled or disassembled equipment, a veritable electronic junkyard.

Bright boy, Juan Carlos.

I found his bag under his bed, which was just as easy for me. Brian's sat in his closet and offered no challenge at all.

My illicit task done, I left Brian's apartment and headed back to Xavier's lab, congratulating myself. You take life's victories where you can.

My route took me past the offices of station security.

***

Christine Bauer was talking to Kanti. I couldn't get close enough to hear the conversation. I didn't dare tell the AI to pipe it over to me. So I watched from behind some old classification manuals perched on the top of a filing cabinet.

Here were two women I admired, so it upset me a little to know they were arguing. Moreover, I was frustrated because I wasn't able to hear what the argument was about. I could hear snippets of conversation as the AI did his best to translate incomplete sentences and ideas.

Maybe the old curiosity thing is true.

The conversation reached a climax when Kanti started shaking her fist at Christine. It was at that moment I detected a different scent. It was another Human female.

My sharp eyes swept all around the office It was not that small as station working spaces go, yet it was packed with three desks, six chairs, filing cabinets, and a rack of servers connected to the three holoterminals.

Some time ago, the AI explained to me that he isn't connected to the security computers. They are connected instead to various UNSA Security installations, on Earth and also on Luna's Farside, Mars, and some research sites beyond.

It was behind the rack of data servers that I spotted Natasha Klachevski. She was trying to listen to the conversation too. When Kanti left in a huff—cat heaven knows what for—Natasha smiled.

We both waited until Christine left the office some twenty minutes later. I tried to follow Natasha but she lost me.

Why was she in Christine's office? I asked myself. *What is she up to that requires she hide?*

***

With the bugs, we soon learned about the Fearsome Four's plan. I was proud of their cleverness in devising a way to follow me. I told Xavier I hated to deceive them.

"Nonsense," he said. "They're only meddlesome children. We can't let them ruin our projects."

"You mean you can't let them ruin your projects," said the AI. "Mr. Paws is right. It's unethical to deceive them."

But when Juan Carlos and Rafael were finished with the device, Xavier easily designed a scrambler for it because we already knew the beacon's exact characteristics. The scrambler turned on and off with a swipe of my paw.

That sleep-cycle, after receiving my usual fix of petting, Shashi picked me up and put me down in the corridor in front of the door to their apartment. I knew the other kids were inside. I was pleased to receive so much attention.

I put my paws to the job at hand. I took off along the corridor with the scrambler off, just to have some fun with them. With their receiver, they followed me, this time at a greater distance than the first time when Shashi had attempted it alone.

At a point when they were out of sight, I swiped at the switch on the scrambler, turning it on, and made my way back to Xavier's lab. He was listening to the Fearsome Four's comments via the bugs.

"Completely mystified," he said with a chortle. "I daresay this is ripe old fun."

"Perhaps," said the AI, "though still unethical."

Chapter Twenty-One

Shashi cast an accusatory look at Juan Carlos. He shrugged.

"I can't figure out where the interference comes from," he said. "Someone's jamming the beacon. It's not a very powerful signal and not terribly wideband, but it's enough to bury our beacon's waveform."

Rafael leaned away from Shashi's student desk, now filled with equipment. Sitting beside Juan Carlos, he had been studying the RF environmental hard copy. He had to look around Shashi to see Brian and Susan, sitting on the bed. Shashi was looking over their shoulders at the tracking equipment electronics and enjoying Rafael's aftershave.

"It's as if they knew our specs exactly," said the astrophysicist. "Their center frequency coincides exactly with ours and their bandwidth is just slightly larger. Guys, this is very suspicious."

"How did they know what frequency to jam at?" said Shashi.

"Good question," said Brian. "Are they bugging us?"

"You mean planting bugs on you?" said Rafael. "That's paranoid. We're not exactly spies, you know."

"What kind of bugs would they use?" said Shashi. With Rafael close enough to touch and Brian not far away, concentrating on the problem at hand was difficult. In fact, at that moment in her tiny bedroom, she had no concern for the cat at all.

Rafael held up two fingers, the space of a small coin between them, and Juan Carlos nodded. "They can be very small. Even the old technology. We'd better check."

They all patted themselves down. Soon Susan pulled a small disk that looked like a watch battery out of her backpack.

The rest checked their bags. Soon Juan Carlos was holding four small disks.

Rafael took them and put a finger to his lips, warning them not to talk. He pulled an aluminum can of table tennis balls out of Juan Carlos' pack he'd seen when his friend was rummaging around inside. Emptying the two balls contained in it into the pack, he put the bugs into the can and put the lid back on. "Now we can talk."

"This is starting to look like Brian's conspiracy theory," said Juan Carlos.

"I wish it wasn't," said Brian. "How do we avoid jamming without letting them know we know they're jamming?"

"When it goes on, can we triangulate it?" said Susan.

"Brilliant!" said Rafael. "We need two more receivers."

"That's easy," said Juan Carlos, and Rafael nodded. "Here's what we'll do."

Shashi refocused. As she listened to the plan, her smile grew broader.

***

Ruthie, Christine, and Kanti were all crowded into Christine's office. Christine was at her video terminal. The other three stood behind her, Ben in the middle, with one arm around Kanti. She didn't seem to mind.

"Watch," said Christine.

They waited as the video terminal painted three holographic images. The first was a still 3D image of Shashi in her gym outfit. That outfit was skimpy but the norm for females working out in the torture chamber. The second was a figure dressed in black tights from head to toe going through seductive motions. She had strapped sensors on all over the figure. The third showed how the still 3D image morphed onto the black figure.

"It's a fake," said Kanti.

Ruthie and Christine nodded.

"I knew it," said Ben. "The question is: who did it? It's not very sophisticated, is it?"

"Not something one does every day, but you're right. It's old technology first used in movies in the late 20th and early 21st centuries," said Christine. "That's why it took me and the AI a while to pin it down. As for who did it, do you have any ideas? Who would want to hurt you, Ben, or Shashi, for that matter?"

Ben looked into Kanti's bright eyes.

"I wish I knew," he said.

***

Someone then called Ruthie out of the office, leaving Christine alone with Ben and Kanti.

Christine swung around in her chair and studied her friends. They were now perched on the edge of the desk that was behind Christine's.

They make a nice couple. I wonder why they don't get hooked up.

She was still working on the case of discrepancies in the GenCorp shipments. In theory, the doctor could be involved, although she had denied it in Christine's office.

Based on that denial and her trust in the doctor, Christine made a decision to assume Kanti was not involved in either the smear campaign or the discrepancies. She had hopes Kanti and Ben would help her solve both cases.

So, holding them to absolute secrecy, Christine told them the story.

"All this might be related to Shashi's porno film," said Christine as she finished.

"Please don't call it that," Kanti said. "Moreover, why discredit Ben or Shashi? What do they have to do with the shipments?"

"Nothing, but you do. You do research for GenCorp."

"I told you before I don't have much to do with who pays the bills," said Kanti. "UNSA takes care of that. The research has gone on here at the station for a long time. It's mostly statistical, as is most medical research. We have many generations of accumulated data, going all the way back to U.S. astronauts and Russian cosmonauts. Even to ESA personnel."

"No one can gain anything by discrediting you or your research?"

"I have no idea who or how or what they'd gain by it. Are discrepancies in the shipments related to my research?"

"As a matter of fact, no. We've been able to unravel what some of the equipment is, though."

"Don't leave us breathless," said Ben.

"It's related to genetic research or gene splicing, I think. Some other shipments are labeled 'live specimens.'"

Ben looked at Kanti, a flash of wonder passing between them. Christine's sharp eye caught it.

"Both outgoing and incoming?" said Ben.

"Not the equipment."

"But live specimens?"

"Yes. Some even shipped out on big rigs. Any ideas?"

Ben looked again at Kanti and Christine could tell he was waiting for her to say something.

"No," she said finally. "However, if we have any, we'll let you know. There might not be any connection with the video either. I think Ben is the real victim on that one."

"Which reminds me," said Ben, "can I return to my teaching?"

"OK by me," said Christine. "I'll have Ruthie put out a general bulletin. That will make the students happy."

"But maybe not the parents," said Ben.

Chapter Twenty-Two

As a driver in some of the major capitals of the world, Rafael Franchetti had suffered greatly. Learning his way around the 3D labyrinth that comprised the International Space Station was easy by comparison. He also had mastered the shuffle required to get around. Once he made the decision to visit Ruthie's office, it took him little time to arrive there.

Rafael looked under the sliding door to the office and saw darkness behind it. Satisfied, he opened the door by punching in the code he had obtained by hacking into Alvaro's files, and shut it behind him. Finally, he turned the lights on.

He checked his watch.

He knew Ruthie's standard issue desktop terminal offered nothing that could help him in his quest. It connected to the station's AI and intranet. As a bureaucrat, he figured she used very little of its visualization horsepower so loved by the station's scientists.

He was looking for another terminal, the one connected to UNSA Security. That was surely more interesting.

Christine's office was too busy because it was always occupied, even in sleep cycles. Here it was easier to try to break into that security system. He also had a chance for more time because Ruthie was often away from her office for long periods.

It was logical Ruthie would swing around in her desk chair and access the security terminal. He felt along the wall behind the chair and found a button recessed into the metal. After pressing it, a panel slid open, revealing not one, but two terminals.

That's confusing, he thought. *Why two?*

He flipped them both on. The one on the left booted with the UNSA logo and said "SPACENET—Authorized Users Only." A paragraph in 10-point font laid out the charges (up to fifty years in prison) and fines (several lifetime's worth of an intern's salary) an illegal user might suffer. Rafael ignored the warnings.

The right terminal was a direct link to the station's AI that gave the user administrative privileges. He found that curious but uninteresting.

Both terminals had an old-fashioned keyboard people now only used for data entry. However, there was no mike nor cad cam, both needed by audio-visual software.

These terminals are old, functioning classics from a by-gone era. Like Ruthie? No, even she's not that old!

Taking a guess, he typed first RuthEllen for the password on the left terminal. When that didn't work, he typed Ruthie. He was in. He had figured she'd have an easily remembered password—after all, the terminal was hidden behind a panel.

The first files he copied were all those pertaining to the missing shipments between the space station and GenCorp, the ones Christine had forwarded to Ruthie. Next, he quickly ran a search through Ruthie's files on Rafael Franchetti, copied those files, and logged out.

As he went out the door, he checked his watch again.

About five minutes. Anyone would be hard pressed to be quicker.

***

As he shuffled back to his office, he was wondering how the Fearsome Four were doing with their plan.

Now there's a quartet for you. Each one smart and each one different. They're definitely on a mission.

So was he. Senator Martinez had made him very uncomfortable at dinner. The embarrassing heroic accolades were partly responsible for his feelings, although it went beyond that. He also knew his compatriot was an international scoundrel. Moreover, he hadn't liked the way the Senator had looked at Shashi. There was still even more to it, though.

Both Martinez and MacGregor had been studying him as if he was some kind of freak in an amusement park. Given that their only connection seemed to be UNSA, he had decided to find out why they were so interested. He was willing to bet it wasn't for his skills as an astrophysicist. Finally, his little excursion was part of a job Dr. Isha Bai, Director of UNSA, had asked him to do back on Earth. *Does Ruthie suspect something?*

He remembered the meeting well. Director Bai had flown on scramjet to London and met with him in a conference room at Cambridge. It was a long ways to go to talk to a lowly astrophysics intern. He later learned she had also addressed the Royal Society, deflating his ego.

The powerful Director of the entire solar system's space exploration and research efforts was tiny but otherwise looked like any other executive from a multinational corporation. Rafael was intimidated at first but warmed up to her.

She spent some time discussing his research plans. He assumed that was politeness, because she didn't waste much time getting down to business.

"Your post-doc is special, you know." He nodded. "Nevertheless, in addition to all the science we've talked about here, there is something else which explains why I wanted to talk to you before you go up to LEO."

"I was wondering about that," Rafael said. "I'm flattered you know about my research with the Kelsos and our desire to continue it. Still, you are a big-picture person. So, let's get out of the weeds."

"Perceptive...and egotistical. You remind me of myself, many years ago. Continuing, without any extra pay—what we're paying you is enough—you will be working for me as well as the Kelsos. They're not to know about our little arrangement, by the way."

"Which is?"

She explained, briefly and precisely, what she wanted. He agreed.

"You realize that if you're caught, I'll deny we ever had this conversation," she said. He still signed on. It was the right course of action.

Back at his office, he was jolted out of his reverie. Shashi was waiting for him, leaning against the office door.

***

"It's going down next sleep cycle," said Shashi in a whisper. "You've been a big help. Want to watch?"

"I have some computer work to do." When she looked disappointed, he felt bad. "You can tell me all about it day after tomorrow. How 'bout we meet in the caf for lunch? I'll buy you all desserts, even if you find out some shuttle pilot smuggled an ordinary house cat in for one of the people here."

"Do you think that's what the cat's story is?"

"I don't know what to think. The wi-fi connections on the cat are hard to explain."

"I think this is one special cat." She stretched tall and planted a kiss on his cheek. "That's for helping us. You're about the only adult who thinks we're not nuts."

He sensed her body heat and wondered if she was trying to be seductive. She was doing a good job of it even if not intentionally. For a brief moment he imagined being with her, but then shook himself out of his daydream. *Shashi, Shashi, you are going to drive some young man crazy.*

"I'm not sure about that," he said. "We're all nuts in some ways, some more than others. Good luck."

"Oh, we won't need it. This plan is a good one." She spun in the low gravity and headed back along the narrow corridor.

Rafael rubbed his cheek, smiled, and went inside.

***

As Shashi shuffled along the corridor, she struggled to bring her emotions under control. The kiss she had given Rafael was timid and without passion. *Why didn't you plant it right on the lips, stupid?* A more passionate kiss would have been an honest expression of her emotions. *But do I want to signal those emotions?*

Rafael was intelligent and well spoken. From what she had seen of him in the torture chamber and elsewhere, he had the body of a soccer player—muscular, limber, and strong, and without those bulging, freaky muscles many men think impress women. She could become lost in those blue eyes that danced with Latino mischief.

She shivered but not from cold. Only months ago, she couldn't have understood her emotions. Now she knew what was happening. She was both embarrassed and intrigued.

Sometimes I feel this way with Brian. Yet Rafael is special.

The corridor lights dimmed behind her and lit beside her, an automatic response during the sleep-cycle. It seemed her thoughts were following her. Scared and confused, she came to a dead stop and wildly looked around, half expecting a tall and sinister figure to appear around the next bend.

Why is growing up so difficult? Why can't adults be more understanding? And why is that damn cat so hard to track?

She pounded on the walls of the corridor in frustration.

"Are you frustrated?" said the AI via her wi-fi implant.

"Yes, I am, you lobotomized abacus." She searched the ceiling and found the unblinking eye of the videocam. "Are you spying on me?"

"I only wanted to have a conversation. I know you're trying to find the cat."

"How do you know anything about it?"

"I'm sorry. I can't answer that question. However, I have analyzed the probabilistic scenarios and decided to warn you: you may be disappointed. You should probably desist."

"Why would I want to do that?"

"To avoid disappointment."

"You yourself said the cat is special. I want to know everything about him and the person who takes care of him."

"Yes, I can understand that. However, you could be disappointed. Some secrets are meant to stay secrets."

"AI, sometimes you're a very meddlesome and ornery computer."

"Shashi, sometimes you're a very meddlesome and ornery young woman."

"Leave me alone. Go suck vacuum."

"I understand the first. The second makes no sense. Still, *ciao bambina.*"

She shuffled on, alone with her thoughts and emotions.

***

After two hours of studying the files from Ruthie's computer, Rafael discovered something he found troubling. There was very little on Martinez, for example, which wasn't unusual, considering the origin of the files. The shipping files were beyond boring.

Only part of one text file caught his eye. He brushed back his unruly mop of blond curls and read the text file again, more slowly this time.

An old news bulletin went back many years. For some reason Ruthie had kept it. The news had appeared on the social pages of the electronic version of the Buenos Aires newspaper *La Prensa*. It was mainly about Dr. Isha Bai and her future plans for financing UNSA. She was speaking at an international conference held in the port city.

He read again the one line that had captured his attention: "Other Space Conference attendees were Senator Fabio Martinez from the Mid Atlantic Union and General Ruth Ellen MacGregor from the Singapore Space Command Center (picture at left)." The picture showed a much younger Martinez and MacGregor. The tiny woman barely had enough room on her breast for the medals she wore. The ugly troll was planting a kiss on her forehead.

Isn't that interesting? thought Rafael. Ruthie and Fabio have a history.

He stretched back in his chair and sighed. He would have to pursue the Ruthie and Fabio connection more.

This spy business is difficult.

Chapter Twenty-Three

"They've been awfully quiet since we last evaded them," said Xavier. "Why don't we hear them?"

"I'm receiving nothing," said the AI. "Mr. Paws, you'll have to check their electronic bugs tonight. If necessary, you can replace them. We have plenty."

"Hey, I'm doing all the physical work," I said in protest. "If Xavier built them poorly, it's not my fault. Maybe we should call it quits."

"Don't be naïve," said Xavier. "They probably left their school bags somewhere. AI, can you determine where those four miscreants are located right now?"

"The bags are at the gym. The Fearsome Four are working out."

"It's too late for that. And it's odd you don't hear the exercise machines."

"I calculate the bugs are too far away from the kids and the machines," said the AI. "When they finish, we will hear them again."

"Or maybe they figured this is a way to plan without us hearing them," said Xavier. "Mr. Paws, jump into the duct work above the gym and see what's going on."

"Oh, dog breath, and just when I wanted to take a catnap," I said, heading off with my tail swishing in the air to let him know I was upset.

I had been to the torture room several times to watch both adults and kids work out. It was an interesting spectacle. Humans sweat a lot. Cats don't.

Of course, Humans are generally disgusting creatures. At best, they only bathe once a day. They also need a source of water, which means they're generally a smelly bunch on the space station, where water is at a premium.

Me, I use my tongue and thus supply my own water. My fur is always in tip-top condition. First class, I'd say.

Shashi and her mother always smell nice, though. They have a special smell I recently etched into my memory. So I knew Shashi wasn't in the gym. Yet their bags were there by their lockers.

I scratched my ear, puzzled by their behavior. *Maybe they're on to us?*

***

That evening began like the previous one. Shashi put a new beacon on me as a goodnight present and sent me off along the corridor leading away from her apartment.

I rounded the corner of the corridor and turned the jamming transmitter on. I made my way back to the secret lab where I scratched at the door.

The door swished open and then closed behind me. I jumped onto a lab stool where I started to wash my face. In a moment I stopped. Xavier was glaring at me as if he were contemplating my demise in numerous unpleasant ways.

"Easy boss—they'll call it quits," I said to Xavier. "Maybe tonight will be their last attempt."

"Shashi's stubborn," said Xavier, lifting me off the stool. "Where are they?" He looked worried but, to his credit, he started to pet me. I suppose it soothed his nerves.

"I don't know," said the AI. "I have no signal. Just a lot of background noise."

I really didn't care. I was starting to get bored with the whole business. I saw a number fly by on a lab instrument's readout and began a mental search for its prime number decomposition. It was an interesting number.

***

The number soon yielded up some of its mysteries. Xavier and the AI were still trying to find out what the Fearsome Four were doing. Because I couldn't find another number nearly as interesting (Xavier must have reset the range of the readout), I decided to play along.

As we waited, I thought it was as good a time as any to ask Xavier about Orson.

"He's fine," said the scientist.

"He's lonely," I said.

"So what? Many lab animals are lonely. We still need them in order to make research progress."

"You need them, you mean," I said. "You make money off them."

"Hardly. Martinez pays me very little. I receive more funding than Kanti, of course, because my research is more important. But I do it out of scientific curiosity, not for the money. Of course, there's the practical side too."

"Like what? Are you going to stop the sun from going nova? Are you going to intercept an asteroid before it hits Earth?"

"What are you talking about? My work is to adapt Earth organisms to different planetary environments. It will be very important when man begins to explore space more. The details of this work are highly classified by the way, so don't blab about it to anyone."

"People wouldn't believe me even if I told them. They'd think the AI here was making it all up." I raised my tail a little to pass some gas. Sometimes Xavier was careless and left my food out—in this case a tin of syntho mackerel—so it became a little hard to digest, to say the least. I was more discreet than Xavier, though, who often did a real number on himself. "And maybe the work is highly classified to hide your many failures. What about me? Am I one of your failures? Or my bird-dog friend?"

"Too many questions," said Xavier. "You don't even know what you're asking." He put me on the floor, probably hoping I'd go away.

***

We concluded the Four had given up. Xavier sat at his lab bench and plunged into deep thought.

That's when I decided to take Orson out for a stroll. I was tempted to let all of Xavier's animals loose, at least the ones that didn't need to be in a tank of water. It would serve him right. I restrained myself. I only opened my friend's cage.

"What's the gig, cat?" said the bird-dog. "We going somewhere to crash? Wanna get away from old Xavier and his bad karma?"

"Stop talking like a twentieth century beat poet. Alan Ginsberg you're not." I shook my tail at him. "And keep quiet, fool. Xavier's now engrossed in his research, but he could hear us."

I jumped onto some crates and pushed back a grill covering an air vent. Orson didn't bother with the crates. He watched me scramble into the duct and then flew up, squeezing through the opening.

"I forgot how big you are," I said. "Don't fluff your feathers in here, Orson, or you'll get stuck. Don't think I'm strong enough to free you either."

I wanted to show him some of the sights. He spent too much time cooped up in a cage.

We first went to the Sky Lounge.

"Is that Earth?" he said.

It was an impressive site. The continent of Africa was below. Off its west coast a tropical storm was brewing. A hurricane was already in the middle of the Atlantic heading for the leeward islands. The planet was perched against a backdrop of an inky black curtain punctuated with brilliant points of light. The view made me feel small. I wondered how it would affect the bird-dog.

"You betcha," I replied. "Mostly water. The ice caps are starting to recover a little from global warming."

"It's beautiful," said the bird-dog. He gave a low woof, which the AI interpreted as a sigh. "And so many stars! You can hardly see them on Earth due to the pollution."

"Depends, I suppose. I think that in the mountains at high altitude they are almost as clear and bright as here. I've never been there, though."

"I really appreciate this, my cat friend. It makes it worthwhile to resist the urge to chase you."

"Good. Now you have to take the nap of my neck and fly me up to the duct."

We continued on our stroll.

Chapter Twenty-Four

Xavier and company's puzzlement was justified. What had happened was Juan Carlos and Rafael had turned the tables.

They had used three receivers to capture Xavier's signal from the jammer that was jamming the beacon. After excising the narrowband signal from the jamming signal on each receiver, the remaining signal from each receiver was pairwise cross-correlated on Susan's tablet computer. Locating the subsequent peaks, she used algorithms she had written to pin down the cat's location within a fraction of a meter. Xavier and company didn't suspect.

This took them some time. After the algorithms spit out the answer giving the cat's location starting from the time the jammer had been turned on, they all rushed through dark corridors to where Susan's equations predicted the cat's last location was. It was solid wall.

"You have the wrong algorithms," said Shashi. Her face was red from more than the run. She thought Susan was incompetent.

"They're fine," said Susan. "You checked them yourself. Get off my back, space witch."

"There has to be some source of error," said Juan Carlos. He didn't care about smoothing over the two girls' squabble—he thought they were being immature. He pounded on the wall.

"Hey, wake the whole place, why don't you?" said Brian.

Their nerves were all frayed by the tension of the moment. They'd been outsmarted at every turn.

Brian was also becoming distracted by seeing Shashi dash around in a skimpy nightshirt. She always looked good, especially in Shimmer. This was different.

She was between him and the light at the end of the corridor. It was enough to see her silhouette. He wondered what she looked like in the video he had heard about.

Her next comment snapped him back to reality.

"Maybe there's a secret door."

"We can't ask the AI to consult station plans," said Susan. "We'll get his same answer: 'I can't answer that question.' We'll have to wait 'til tomorrow."

"I'm starting to lose patience," said Shashi. "The cat can't just disappear."

"Cat's are fast," said Juan Carlos, "and this one's used to low gravity. He may be too quick for us."

They agreed to call it a night. All except Brian.

***

Shashi, Susan and Juan Carlos headed home. Their quarters were close to each other, while Brian's was on the other side of the station where Ben and many scientists lived.

"I can't figure it out," said Shashi. "There must be something behind that wall. But how can there be?"

"It must be in the plans," said Susan. "Otherwise, how can Alvaro and his people service it?"

"Maybe whoever is behind that wall takes care of that," said Juan Carlos. "And they take care of the cat. Maybe Alvaro doesn't know anything is there."

They turned a corner in the corridor. Susan, in the lead, emitted a scream and threw up her hands to protect her face. The cat ran between her legs. He was followed by a flying monstrosity beating its wings vigorously.

Juan Carlos and Shashi threw themselves on the floor. Shashi whipped out her cell phone and snapped pictures as the strange pair turned the same corner in the corridor going the other way.

"Were we just attacked by an ET?" said Susan.

"Maybe an encounter, not an attack," said Shashi, studying her pictures. "I think you'll recognize the bird-dog from Shimmer."

"It's real," said Juan Carlos.

"Or a triple hallucination," said Shashi. She stood and ran after the duo.

After a few seconds, she shuffled back to them, disappointment on her face. "No sign of them. Didn't we just follow that damn cat to that solid wall?"

"No one's dreaming," said Juan Carlos. "And that was some time ago. I'd rather have caught the cat with that avian creature. It can clear us a lot with Christine and Ruthie for that Shimmer caper that KO'd the AI."

"We figured that wasn't real," said Susan. "Now we know it sort of was. The real-life creature is about the scariest thing I've ever experienced."

"You have to watch more old movies," said Juan Carlos. "Take a look at one titled *Alien*. Now, there was a real monster."

***

"I think you'll want to see this," said Christine, after sitting in Ruthie's low chair designed to put guests in her office at the small woman's same level.

"Not more porno, I hope," said Ruthie.

"On the contrary, you will recall the whole incident with the kids' game and the shutdown of the AI."

Ruthie nodded. *How could I not? I saved the day with my dedicated terminal. How careless of Xavier!* She waited for

148

more words from Christine, who was busy transferring a video file over to Ruthie's standard issue holoterminal.

Most personnel knew the AI kept video surveillance on all the station's inner corridors. It was a safety procedure long ago established by UNSA Security as the number of people on board grew over the decades into the hundreds. Security rarely looked at the files, though, unless there was some other circumstance where they might be useful. They usually wiped them on a regular basis.

"Dr. Garcia was not answering calls last night so I was trying to locate her. Brenda Rice came down with appendicitis. It turns out the doctor's phone had dead batteries. She didn't realize it."

"My lord, Brenda has an appendix?"

"Some people still do. It's a rarity, I'll agree."

"Is she all right?"

"She will be. Kanti is setting up for surgery now." She reached over and hit a VIEW button on Ruthie's machine. "That only explains why I looked at the files. In my search I came across this."

Ruthie watched the video unfold. It was distorted. *Dirty lens?* Still, it was clear enough to show three of those four meddlesome children.

She sucked in her breath as the cat and the bird-dog came running along the corridor. There was a change of cameras producing a glitch. The next video clip showed the bird-dog lifting the cat into the ductwork by the scruff of its neck.

"What was that?" said Ruthie, although she already knew.

"I'm not quite sure how to interpret it. That beast and cat are exactly as the kids described them in their computer game."

Xavier, I'm going to have your hide! And that cat and bird-dog have to go!

"Christine, I think you need to have a talk with these children. Is it possible they doctored this video? They're way too smart for their own good, you know."

"I find that hard to believe. I guess it's possible. I hate to accuse them. We found out that Shashi was innocent in the porno case."

I figured you'd say that, thought Ruthie. *The bleeding hearts are always concerned about the kids, no matter how scheming and mischievous they become.*

"OK, keep your investigation as quiet as you can. I want to know who doctored that video. Maybe it's the same joker that mucked around with the kids' game."

Nice cover-up, at least for now. Ruthie knew it was a temporary fix. *How it all pans out is anyone's guess. Damn that Xavier!*

***

At the same time Christine chatted with Ruthie, Brian knocked on Ben's door. The teacher opened it.

"Hey, Brian, what's new? It's kind of late into the sleep-cycle for you, isn't it?" Ben was dressed in sweat shorts and sandals. He held a squirt bulb of Irish whiskey in his hand. "Are you alone? I'd have you in but I'm in the middle of preparing classes for tomorrow."

"I need to know if it's true about you and Shashi," said Brian.

"Who told you?"

"So it's true!"

Ben saw Brian making fists.

"No, it's not true. Christine Bauer has proven the video is a fake."

"I haven't seen any video. I heard about it, though. I also heard you can't teach anymore because you, uh, took advantage of Shashi."

"What you heard was wrong. Classes as usual tomorrow, my friend." He paused a moment. Brian knew there were more words coming and became uncomfortable. "How can you believe Shashi and I could do something like that?" Ben finally said. "What kind of people do you think we are?" Brian knew his face was slowly reddening. "Oh, I get it. You have a thing for Shashi. Kids! I still need to know who told you. I'll pass it on to Christine."

"I'm not going to snitch on anyone," said Brian.

"OK. Do it your way. I think you're making a big mistake."

Ben shut the door, leaving Brian alone in the corridor.

***

The next door Brian knocked on was Rafael's. On the way to the astrophysicist's quarters, Brian received the pictures of the bird-dog and the cat from Shashi on his phone.

The door opened. One of Rafael's roomies rubbed his eyes as he looked out at Brian.

"Hey, Kelso, you have some nerve. We're trying to sleep in here, you know."

"I need to talk to Rafael."

"I'll get him, but you'll have to talk out there. We all have a full schedule and need our beauty sleep. Not like you station brats."

Brian knew there was some animosity between the younger station personnel and those still attending school. He ignored the barb and simply nodded.

Soon Rafael joined him in the corridor. As the door whooshed shut, he slid down the wall, using it for back support, and sat on the floor. Brian joined him.

"Any luck?"

"No, we can't figure it out. The cat disappeared. Maybe Susan's algorithms are wrong. We decided to split and go home." He handed his phone to Rafael. "The other three had a run in with the cat and the bird-dog."

"From the game? I thought you guys weren't supposed to play it anymore?"

"A live run-in. The bird-dog's as real as the cat."

Rafael rolled his eyes. "If you were any older, I'd think you've had strong drink or were smoking something." He gave back the phone. "Video records can be doctored, you know."

"My friends wouldn't doctor the pictures, and I'm clean from drugs. I don't know about the other three."

"Susan and Juan are too uptight to do drugs. Shashi's high strung, all right, but I don't think she does any stuff either. Isn't she a member of that weird sect?"

"It's not a sect. It's a brand new religion some Spacers follow. She's pretty serious about it. Not to mention that her mom has come to class many times to educate us about medical hazards. Shashi won't do drugs. You're way out of line, friend."

Rafael only nodded. Brian figured he had come down too hard on him. Brian looked at his hands while Rafael waited for more.

"I need girl advice," Brian finally said.

"Aha. You've come to the right man."

"You've had lots of girlfriends?"

"Enough to know being high strung is the least of your worries with Shashi. She's into older men."

Brian didn't think to ask how Rafael knew it was Shashi. He was more worried the "older man" might be Rafael. "How old?"

"I'm guessing she's already had a crush on Ben but probably recognizes she can't compete with her mother. She's also made eyes at me."

"So, do you like young women?"

"Come on, Brian, she's only thirteen. While I'm flattered, she's too young. She's all yours, my friend."

"I wish," said Brian. "She's a good friend. I don't think she sees me as a romantic interest."

Rafael laughed. "Oh, you might be surprised. Give her some time. I've noticed you two snap at each other a lot. You both need to soften the rhetoric."

"I'm not sure I understand that advice."

"I'm not sure I do either," said Rafael, standing, "but it sounded good. Don't argue so much with her and do nice things occasionally." He stretched and yawned. "Now, I do need to get some sleep. You do too." He offered a hand to Brian and pulled the boy to his feet. "Remember we have a life expectancy of 120 now and it's creeping up all the time. You'll have plenty of time to get to know girls, even if you only date Spacers. I'm still waiting for the right one myself. We have to be patient."

Brian nodded and thanked the astrophysicist for the chat.

"Juan Carlos might look you up. We need an alternate plan."

"Sounds interesting," said Rafael. "I'd like to help."

Chapter Twenty-Five

Soon after I left on my stroll with Orson, Xavier and the AI heard the Fearsome Four pounding on the door to the secret lab. When I returned, I managed to sneak the bird-dog in without anyone knowing. I smoothed my fur a little and then sauntered out into view. I sat on my haunches and continued to wash my face.

"They found us," said Xavier, who was pacing up and down in front of the main door. "That quartet is ruining everything."

"They found a wall," said the AI. "They have no idea what's behind it. They can't get in without your code."

"I'm not taking any chances," said Xavier. "We'll block the main door and start using the other one."

"I wonder how they did it," I said, happy the AI had not ratted me out. Maybe he was learning to lie. Or, was it that he didn't offer the truth if no one asked? Some called that a lie by omission. Politicians are good at both.

"I told you they were smart," said Xavier, as he slid a heavy cabinet in front of the main door. "They somehow figured out what we were doing and beat us at our own game. I can't allow this to continue." He went to one of his lab benches and showed them a syringe.

"You can't kill her!" said the AI in a surprising show of human-like caring. I also meowed my protest, knowing he meant Shashi.

"Of course not, you idiots! This will put her down for a week or so. Either by caring for her or becoming sick herself, Kanti will be out of action too. That will give me time to work something else out."

"You're diabolical," I said.

Xavier smiled like a devilish fiend. "Thanks for the compliment."

***

I took the coward's way out and told Xavier I didn't want to know when he was going to perform the black deed, only after he did it. He agreed. *Why not?* He was in charge and probably preferred not to let the AI or me know anything more about his detailed plans.

During the next wake-cycle, however, Xavier wasn't successful in finding Shashi. I was sad when I learned in the next one he succeeded in his plan. I wondered what was in the syringe.

"I walked by her on her way to school," he said. "She had her mind on her classes. She didn't know. Now, we have some serious planning to do." He picked me up and put me in a cage. "That's the first step. No more visiting with the little brat either."

"I object," I said, hissing and spitting. "Have you gone crazy?"

"I also protest," said the AI. "Mr. Paws is our friend."

"And that's my mistake," said Xavier. "I was lulled into complacency and forgot my mission. You two are not friends! You are my creations—I own you."

The flow of air stopped and the lights dimmed.

"I can turn off the oxygen and power to your lab," said the AI.

"And kill Mr. Paws, Helldog, and my other guests?" he said, pointing to the other room behind the locked door that contained specimens. "I don't think you have the guts."

"You're right. I don't. I can do something else. I can refuse to help you. Goodbye, Xavier."

My ability to communicate with Xavier via the wi-fi device disappeared. Now I was just another lab animal.

Xavier had gone off the deep end. The AI now refused to talk to him. When Xavier ripped off his wi-fi device, I knew he couldn't communicate with the AI either.

***

Orson's cage was across the aisle and two down from mine. His was bigger. He didn't have room to fly although he could stretch out his wings.

He barked at me. Although I knew it was a greeting, without the AI we couldn't understand each other. He was wagging his tail, probably recalling our stroll.

"So you two beasties are friends," said Xavier, stopping at Orson's cage and looking into the eyes of my intelligent friend. Although I couldn't communicate with either Xavier or Orson, I could understand what Xavier was saying. "Helldog, say goodbye, *hasta la vista, sayonara, ciao*. You won't be seeing Mr. Paws again. It's time you start earning your pay."

Xavier shook a can of something—it looked like paint —and sprayed some of its contents into Orson's face. My bird-dog friend keeled over, unconscious. I protested.

"Oh, shut up," said Xavier, tired of my strident yowls and spitting, "or I'll give you the same just to keep you quiet. It's harmless—he's only taking a nap."

I calmed down. I knew I was wasting energy. Xavier's tone wasn't threatening. I just didn't like being in a cage. Or, seeing Orson knocked out on the bottom of his cage. Right then, there was nothing I could do.

Later, I watched Xavier take Orson's sleeping body out of the cage and place it on some straw in a shipping crate. He went back to the main lab and returned with some labels.

I could understand what he wrote:

GenCorp Proprietary
To: Europa Station
GenCorp Chief Scientist Dr. William Bradford
FOR YOUR EYES ONLY
From: Dr. Boris Petrovich, ISS
HANDLE WITH CARE – LIVE SPECIMEN
GenCorp Proprietary

Next, Xavier put all kinds of official stamps and packing slips on the crate. He then carried it back to the main lab. He spoke into the computer, calling up a program or two.

I couldn't see the screen. I supposed the AI's refusal to talk didn't affect his more primitive functions. Or, Xavier knew how to detour around any block the AI might try to impose on those functions.

I was dumbfounded. It was the first time I saw Xavier prepare a specimen for shipping. It was clear my friend Orson was heading for Europa, one of Jupiter's moons—in particular, a GenCorp research station.

Moreover, to the best of my knowledge, Xavier had used a false name. I knew most everyone at LEO—there was no Boris Petrovich.

My faux friend was showing his true colors. I needed to think of ways to stop him. The fact that I was now his prisoner hindered my coming up with a good plan.

Chapter Twenty-Six

Rafael Franchetti stared at Ruthie's computer monitor.

A little earlier it had occurred to him why Ruth Ellen MacGregor had AI administrative privileges in her office: She could change any of the computer records at will—her own, anyone else's, shipping and security records—they were all accessible to her. He returned to her office and started snooping through her files again.

This time he took longer and was more methodical. He wasn't a hacker, yet he was good enough to trace changes. Now it was clear that over many years the diminutive woman had left a subtle trail of deceit and manipulation.

I have found Dr. Bai's agent, the person responsible for circumventing the usual security checkpoints in order to provide an unfettered path for GenCorp's corporate shenanigans. He licked the nervous sweat from his lips. *Now I understand the photograph in La Prensa. She's always worked with Fabio Martinez.*

He logged out, slid the terminal and its old keyboard back into its recess, and closed the panel.

His own deceit had taken longer than planned. He rose from the uncomfortable chair and shuffled to the door.

As a scientist, I believe in leaps of intuition. It's how the human mind does its best work. His intuition told him this gig was not going to end well. *I'll have to be ready for anything.*

***

"Fancy meeting you here, Dr. Franchetti."

Rafael stared at the gun pointed at his chest. He assumed Christine Bauer knew how to use it. He remained calm.

"What were you doing in my office?" said Ruthie.

"I don't have to answer any of your questions." He looked at Ruthie. "I'm here as a UNSA Science Adjunct, working with the Kelsos. If Christine shoots me in the back, there'll be hell to pay."

Rafael brushed by Ruthie, almost knocking her over, and shuffled along the dark corridor.

"Shoot him!" said Ruthie, hissing like a snake.

Christine put her gun away. "I'm afraid I can't do that. We know he was in your office. There's nothing illegal about his being there. He violated your privacy in some sense, but legally there's no privacy to violate on ISS. The most you can try to do is declare him *persona non grata* and ship him back to Earth." She faced Ruthie's wrath. Ruthie sensed she was going to stroke out. "I think you need a reason for that, too," said Christine, "or the Kelsos will lead a mutiny. What's eating you?"

Ruthie managed to control her anger.

"OK. Technically I'm not his boss, the Kelsos are. Still, I'm your boss, damn it! I want a 24/7 watch on Franchetti. He's up to no good. I bet he's responsible for the AI crash and all the missing shipments. And probably Shashi's porn movie."

Nice touch, old woman, thought Ruthie. *Throw all the blame onto him.*

"We're still waiting for the techie to come from Earth to service the AI. It's clear its problems have something to do with that infernal game the Fearsome Four play." Christine licked her lips, a nervous habit from grade school. "As for the second, the missing shipments have occurred over a long period of time. Franchetti wasn't on board most of that time. I think you're chasing ghosts, Ruthie."

"He wasn't in my office to steal my Earl Grey tea," said Ruthie. She knew she couldn't have Christine dust for prints—the other secret terminal would be exposed. "Like I said, 24/7 watch. By the way, Franchetti is far too chummy with the Fearsome Four. He's probably encouraging them."

"I'll set up a surveillance detail. Now, go get some sleep."

***

Brendan Kelso glanced up from his terminal. "Have a problem, Rafael?" He rubbed sleep out of his eyes and reached for his syntho coffee bulb.

"I have a confession to make," said Rafael. "You probably will be upset by it, but hear me out."

He explained how Dr. Isha Bai, the Director of UNSA, had asked him to do a little extracurricular spy work during his internship aboard the space station. He told Brendan what he had uncovered.

The older astrophysicist patiently listened but started to look uncomfortable at the end. "I find this hard to believe. I've known Ruthie for years. What are these shipments anyway?"

"I can get a list although it might be meaningless. She has the ability to change the listings of contents, including origin and destination. She also has complete control over the AI."

"Which means she could be listening to this conversation?"

"Possibly. I've already been discovered. Moreover, I'm not sure she will try moving against you or your wife, though she can attempt to cover up her handiwork."

"So, what do you want from me?" said Brendan. "I can't see that I can help you. We're administratively independent, as you pointed out to Christine and Ruthie."

"It's possible Ruthie will try to force you and Akasuki to terminate my internship. I'm only asking you not to do that. At least not yet."

"I see. If she'd ask us to do that without our little discussion we would want an explanation, so all this would come out, but with her spin on it. Thanks for keeping us in your confidence. Let me talk to Akasuki. Don't worry. We'll back you."

"I appreciate it." Rafael stood, preparing to leave.

"By the way, we'd have told Ruthie to go eat moon dust anyway. Like I said, no jurisdiction. Next, we'd have asked you why she's after your hide."

***

Ruthie stared at the information on her computer screen. She rubbed her eyes in disbelief.

After digging through many old computer records, she had solved the mystery of why Rafael Franchetti had looked so familiar when she had first studied his file.

She placed his 3D image in one-half of the screen's output and Fabio's in the other half. She then expanded the left image to full size. She rocked them back and forth, viewing the two men's features from different angles.

"I'll be damned," she muttered. *As old as I am, there are always more surprises.*

She had to assume Rafael was working with Isha Bai or someone close to the director.

The next hours will be rough. Can I take it?

Chapter Twenty-Seven

"I haven't seen him since yesterday in the corridor."

The reverb from the nearly empty Sky Lounge amplified the worried tone in Shashi's voice. She was standing tall, leaning against the transparent surface, her forehead resting against the wall, and her feet appearing to stand on stars.

"Maybe he's dead!"

Shashi turned and glared at Juan Carlos.

"Just because he's missing," said Susan, "doesn't mean he's dead." She put a comforting hand on Shashi's shoulder. "Cats often go missing for days."

"Who told you that?" said Juan Carlos. "I heard they only go missing when they go off to die."

"Will you three sorrowful dimwits please stop?" said Brian. Shashi never liked being called names. She still mouthed a silent "thank you" she was sure he saw. "Wild theories are not useful. How many of you have known a cat?" Shashi slowly raised her hand. "I mean, for a long time, not just a few days. And this cat's special. You all saw the wi-fi socket."

Juan Carlos nodded.

"That's true," said Susan. "The AI must know how to communicate with the cat. The bird-dog, my ET, had a socket too."

"Hey, AI, can you speak to the cat?" It was an obvious question that hadn't occurred to Shashi to ask before.

"The cat is incommunicado," said the AI.

"Where is he? Why can't you speak to him?"

"I'm not at liberty to say."

"Don't give me that crap. Do you know where he is?"

"Yes."

"So tell us."

"I'm not at liberty to say."

"Can you speak to him?"

"Yes, but not now. He's not wearing his wi-fi device."

"How do you speak to him?" said Brian, surprise written on his face.

"The same way I speak to you."

"We subvocalize and you receive signals from the wi-fi device. The cat has no language."

"We have a mutual language."

They all thought about that a moment.

"This cat is special, isn't he?" said Shashi.

"He is," said the AI.

They couldn't pry anything more out of the AI about either the cat or the bird-dog, only a lot more statements where he insisted he wasn't able to answer. After more thought, they agreed they needed to attack the problem anew from multiple directions.

***

"We'll find him," Brian said to Shashi.

He had stayed behind as Susan and Juan Carlos left to put the first part of their master plan into action. Shashi, who had been watching the rotating Earth, turned to him.

"You're comforting, although you know as well as I do Juan Carlos could be right." Some tears ran down her cheeks. "He's one person I've ever bonded with and wanted to protect."

Brian sat and put his head on his knees.

"Odd you call him a person. Is that because you now know he talks to the AI?"

"Person, cat-thing, mutant—it doesn't matter. We've bonded. I'm sure of it." She sat beside him in a lotus position. "Call it intuition if you want."

"Do you feel this bond with anyone else?" said Brian, looking off into the infinities captured by the lounge window.

"Only a few. My mother. You guys. Maybe Rafael. I feel it in different degrees with different people. I think the cat expresses unquestioning love for me."

"Maybe those others do too. Like me."

He turned his face toward her and she kissed him. "That's the nicest thing you've ever said to me, Sir Brian."

"And you're the only one I've ever said it to, Maid Shashi."

***

"Finally!" said Christine, walking into Ben's office. She was surprised to find Kanti there. "I know who's slandering you and Shashi and everyone else."

"It's about time," said Kanti. "Male patients are starting to look at me a little strangely. Female ones look at me as if they want to put a stake through my heart, especially the married ones. They know the video's fake and still the rumors are stronger than the video."

"I guess some people have nothing better to do," said Ben. He winked at Kanti. "Even Alvaro, who says he doesn't buy into any of the rumors, asked me if Kanti and I were doing it."

Kanti turned red.

"Forget it, doc," said Christine. "Like Ben said, some people have nothing better to do."

"So, what are you going to do about this person?" said Ben. Christine noticed he was enjoying Kanti's discomfort.

"Confront her. Make her offer a public apology."

"That's tough," said Ben. "But it's probably the best way to end all the gossip."

***

Ruthie's phone rang as she was heading to the Sky Lounge for a power lunch with another corporate sponsor, Senator Denise Andersen, CEO of WorldNet. She looked at the name of the caller and hit the receive button.

"Hi, Christine. Good news?" The young woman was smiling.

"I found our porno producer."

Ruthie noted the security head looked young and beautiful on the small screen of the phone. *And I'm old and withered like an Egyptian mummy. The years don't pass in vain.*

"Please tell me it wasn't someone I respect."

"Depends. A kid, a very clever kid. Natasha Kluchevski. The other kids often call her the Gnat. She and a group of friends formed a little clique that often tries to put down and bully other kids."

"I might get pissed myself if they gave me a nickname like that. Natasha is such a pretty name." She turned a corner in the corridor and stopped at the entrance to the Sky Lounge. "Have you told Ben and Kanti?"

"Affirmative. They were relieved."

"So am I. What are you going to do?"

"Confront Natasha and try to get her to publicly apologize."

"Not easy to do, especially if others in her clique were in on it. But go for it…and good luck."

Ruthie closed the phone. With her short height, she had often been the butt of cruel jokes from other kids. It only toughened her and motivated her to push herself to succeed in everything she tried. Number one at the U.S. Air Force Academy when there was still a United States. First Westerner to become a general in Singapore's Space Command. Youngest and longest running head of ISS.

She realized other kids might react differently.

Now, how much can I take of Senator Andersen?

The Senator had a reputation for appreciating only those persons that catered to her whims. But the tall CEO of WorldNet, with the best body her parents could provide her using modern genetic engineering techniques, was considerate that day. She sat demurely with her legs crossed, sipping an expensive Pinot Grigio and toying with some appetizers.

"Sorry, I'm late, Senator. You cannot believe the distracting interruptions I have to contend with."

And I am distracted. Rafael Franchetti is a major distraction, for example, along with those four meddlesome brats.

Continuing her policy of polite consideration, the golden-skinned beauty made no comment about lateness and simply offered a hand as Ruthie sat.

"My dear Ruthie, think nothing of it. I empathize. I normally field fifty distractions such each hour." She gestured towards the curving transparent wall and half floor that appeared to leave them hanging in space above the blue-green planet below. "That's why I turn all com devices off when I come into this room. I can enjoy my food, drink, conversation, and the loveliest view I've ever seen."

"You should be a Spacer."

"I'm too addicted to power," the powerful woman said. Ruthie was surprised at the confession. The other woman put a small morsel into her mouth. "If I were on Mars or somewhere like that—maybe one of those Earth-like planets that used to make the news—I'd start a revolution and become the Supreme Leader or something." She pointed to the plate. "Try the shrimp. They're excellent."

Ruthie smiled. *My dear, you exhibit self-control though you are full of yourself. I wonder how many glasses of wine it will take to get another billion or so out of you.* She picked up one of the shrimp and dipped it into the cocktail sauce. *And what would dear Fabio say if he knew I was making him compete with Denise?*

***

Shashi came up with the idea that whoever was taking care of the cat had to represent a steady drain on space station supplies, particularly oxygen, water, and food. Not only that, additional waste products, like carbon dioxide and bodily excretions, should also be observable as an additional burden on the recycling system.

She assigned the task of implementing that idea to Juan Carlos and Susan. They used the excuse of a school project to convince Juan Carlos's father to allow them to record and study the appropriate readouts from physical plant.

Neither one mentioned the interchange in Juan Carlos's room when they worked on the Shimmer module. He was all business. She helped the best she could.

It was not an easy task. After a day's work, they had localized the origin of the miniscule changes to a certain area on the station. They were both disappointed when it turned out to be near the blank wall that stymied them in their previous experiment.

***

In that same one-day period, Shashi and Brian confirmed there were shipments going in and out of the docks never registered by the AI. They did this by comparing what went in and out of the spaceport on Earth and the space station, duplicating most of the work Dan Wong and Christine Bauer had already performed. They were also unaware of Rafael's sleuthing—they couldn't even locate the young scientist.

Again, it was hard work. They knew they hit pay dirt when they found a suspicious shipment ready to arrive on an Earth shuttle. The manifest indicated material the space station wasn't supposed to receive. That meant a trip to the shuttle docks to find out what was going on.

The shipment arrived during a sleep-cycle. Shashi and Brian were already there, waiting, watching, and awake, hiding behind an unused loader. Neither had problems sneaking out. All their parents were fast asleep.

They watched the dockworkers help the Downy shuttle crew unload several tons of material and slide most of it onto conveyor belts that carried it into the space station's hub area. They left behind a number of crates on the docks.

***

"This is it," said Shashi in a whisper.

Brian yawned. "I sure hope so. I'm becoming stiff. And bored."

Shashi grabbed his hand and rubbed it vigorously.

"Get with the program," she said. "You can't go to sleep now." She was feeling hot and tired herself although the adrenalin surging in her veins was a stimulant.

Brian draped his free arm across her shoulders.

"It's nice being here with you," he said, his voice a mumble, "but I really need to sleep."

Shashi kissed him. She relished their closeness, even though Brian was half-asleep. She attributed her feverish blush to that—it didn't occur to her she was sick.

She was wiping away drops of perspiration when she heard two "pfft!" sounds and felt the dart sting her neck. She became very sleepy. She noticed Brian had a dart in his neck too. He was already out for the count.

Before her eyes closed, she saw a tall figure who reached across their stiffening bodies and removed the darts. All dressed in black, he looked like a sorcerer, a true manipulator of black magic. She couldn't see the face well. It was in the shadows of a cowl. She had last seen him in a video game.

Now she could see the eyes more clearly. With her fever, they seemed penetrating and malevolent.

***

"What are they doing?" said Susan.

"I think they're sleeping," said Juan Carlos. "Talk about dedication!"

Their task was to provide backup for their friends. Juan Carlos's infrared sensors had registered the lowering of Shashi and Brian's body heat as they went to sleep, although it was puzzling Shashi's temperature was still higher than Brian's.

"Who's that?" said Susan.

A tall, ghostly figure bent down towards their two friends, lifted them one by one, and set them on top of two of the crates. He then began sliding all the remaining crates onto a cart.

He moved out of the dock area, struggling to push the cart on its little wheels at first and then relaxing when it was finally in motion and barely touching the floor. His gait was one of a man accustomed to micro-gravity.

"*Diablos,* he's our guy! Let's go!"

"We can't catch him," Susan said.

"We don't have to. We know where he's going."

They dashed along the darkened corridors towards the wall where they had lost the cat and where Plan A had led them. Plan B had just failed. Plan C was now in effect, being created on the fly.

They arrived in the corridor at the same time as the ghostly figure and his cargo. He struggled to bring the cart to a stop, put his forehead against the wall to open the door, and proceeded to move the cart inside.

Juan Carlos rushed forward before Susan could stop him. He was tugging at Brian, who was more towards the rear of the baggage cart than Shashi, when there was a "pow!"

The leads the ghost shot from a taser struck Juan Carlos in the chest. He fell, shaking in convulsions.

Susan heard the words "meddlesome brats" as she rushed forward. The door whisked shut.

Chapter Twenty-Eight

I was glad to see Shashi again—but not in those circumstances.

When Xavier brought the cart in with my friend, at first I thought she and Brian were dead. But after thinking about it rationally, I decided he'd never bring them back if he'd killed them. And I was sure Xavier wasn't a murderer.

But I also knew he had done something to them, beyond shooting up Shashi with some disease, so I was worried. I paced back and forth in the cage, my back arched and my tail swishing from side to side. I spit out some cursing meows.

He gently placed Shashi and Brian into two desk chairs. I could see them from my cage. He then stored away all he had brought back from the docks.

Although I expressed my dissatisfaction with his actions, he ignored me, content to catalog what he had received and find an appropriate spot for it. He took a few crates into one of the other rooms.

I heard cage doors rattling as he transferred some live specimens from crates to a more humane place, if you can call cages humane.

***

After about a half hour, Shashi started to stir. I could see that Xavier was still busy. She studied her surroundings.

Maybe she can escape, I told myself.

The desk chairs belonged to two desks built into a row of cabinets that had equipment she could only recognize as belonging to a sophisticated lab. She wouldn't know its purpose, though.

She watched Xavier adjusting dials on some of the far machines. He was like a man possessed, oblivious to what my two friends were doing.

She slid off the desk chair, crawled on her belly around the corner of a cabinet, and wriggled towards the door.

"*Halten Sie!*" Footsteps. Xavier's gnarled hand hoisted her by the collar of her school uniform. "*Ach, Fraulein* Garcia."

Sometimes Xavier spoke in German. When he told Shashi to stop in that guttural language and grabbed her, I knew he wasn't pleased. He steadied her. She stared at him, her eyes wide with fear.

"I-I don't know you," she said.

"No, you don't. However, my dear, I know you very well. Kantimati and I were quite the item until your meddlesome father came on the scene. Meddlesome father, meddlesome daughter. Genetics is everything."

"Who are you?" she said. I could see her watching Brian out of the corner of her eye. He too was doing a belly crawl on his way towards the door.

"Call me Dr. X. The X is for Xavier, by the way." His baritone laugh reverberated in the lab. "And *Herr* Kelso, I'd give up slithering like a snake in your effort to escape me. You'll only soil yourself with the lab gook that's on the floor. I'm not very tidy, you see. The door is locked, by the way."

Brian also stood and came towards them.

"I don't know who you are but you'd better let us go. Our parents can cook your goose in many ways."

Xavier chuckled. His bushy eyebrows waggled up and down in time with his chortling.

"Such an old-fashioned cliché. Indeed, have you ever seen a goose, either of you?"

"In video clips," said Shashi, testing his hold on her.

Xavier let her go. She ran to the door and started to pound on it.

"I'm not sure that's going to accomplish much," said Brian.

"Smart boy," said Xavier. He pulled out a pack of oatmeal cookies, took one, and shoved the pack towards them.

Shashi approached warily. The cookies looked good. At the same time, the mere sight of them seemed to make her dizzy.

"What are you doing here?"

"Continuing my work." He chuckled again. To Shashi his laugh must have sounded deranged. It certainly did to me. "They thought they got rid of me in the fire, you see. I fooled them! Then, mystery of all mysteries, when they went to find my files in the computer, they didn't find anything. We'll never let them steal my work." The last was the hissing threat of a venomous serpent.

He only lacks a rattle, I thought, *to be one of those venomous snakes.* My master was even creeping me out.

Shashi looked at Juan Carlos and then at the cookies. She didn't know what to think, I'm sure.

I was still certain Xavier was more an eccentric than a villain, although he often had his bad moments. He went to the refrigerator, which was close to my cage, and pulled out a soy milk carton.

"Can't have cookies without milk, you know."

Shashi spotted me.

"The cat! Why is he in a cage?"

"That's a long story," said Xavier. He put down the milk carton, opened the cage door, and picked me up.

173

Walking over to the cabinet, he found the small wi-fi device he plugged into my head. "Now, if the AI will get out of his damn funk, we can all have a pleasant conversation. Over cookies."

"I want some real milk," I said. My two friends stared at me as if I were magical. "And petting. I'm feeling neglected."

Chapter Twenty-Nine

Natasha glanced first at Christine and then at Ruthie.

"I'm not doing it," said the Gnat. "You can't make me apologize. Anyway, it's my word against Shashi's. It's all Brian's fault. If he were here, I'd scratch his eyes out."

"I'm not sure I understand that," said Ruthie, making a peak out of her hands to rest her chin on as she studied the girl. "This is a serious offense, young lady. UNSA Security could ban you from the station. But since you say it's your word against Shashi's, let's get Shashi in here." She winked at Christine.

"Not a bad idea," said Christine. She picked up her cell phone. She turned her head away so the Gnat couldn't hear the conversation. After a moment, she turned back to the defiant young girl.

"What have you done with Shashi and Brian?" Christine said.

"Nothing," said the Gnat. Christine's eyes bore into her while Ruthie's prayer hands became fists. "I haven't done anything to them, beyond what you accused me of."

"Then why are they missing?" Christine looked at Ruthie. "And how can they be missing? We don't have a lot of real estate here."

***

"You have to come quickly," Juan Carlos told his father. The hand holding his phone trembled. His voice was high-pitched as fear for his friends left more of a mark on him than the residual effects of the taser. "Bring tools and Rafael and some of your guys. Kanti and Ben too."

Alvaro, half asleep, was confused. "Do you know what time it is?"

Susan leaned towards Juan Carlos so Alvaro could also hear her. "It's time to save Brian and Shashi."

Alvaro was immediately awake. "What happened?"

"We'll explain when you arrive," said Juan Carlos.

With the urgent plea from his son, it wasn't surprising Alvaro was the first to arrive. Any other time he would be a comical figure, dressed in pajamas with a tool belt around his waist and pushing a tool cart. The rest of his men came straggling in one-by-one along with Christine, Kanti and Ben. Rafael was not with them.

"This better not be a Fearsome Foursome prank," said Kanti. She then saw the cables from the taser.

"Natasha went way too far," said Ben.

"If she did something to my daughter, I'll put her through the airlock myself," Kanti said.

"Easy," said Alvaro, patting Kanti on the arm. "What's going on?" he said to Juan Carlos.

"I don't think the Gnat has anything to do with this," said Susan. Juan Carlos nodded.

She and Juan Carlos explained everything that had happened. Kanti shuddered when they told her about the darts and the taser.

"It's worse than I thought."

"You should have involved us earlier," said Ben.

"Only Rafael believed us," said Juan Carlos.

***

Alvaro and his men went over every square centimeter of the wall.

"Not a seam. Are you sure this is where they all disappeared?"

"Positive," said Susan. "The ghostly guy would have dragged Juan Carlos in too, but he was twitching on the floor."

"He could have stopped his heart," said Kanti. "Those tasers are usually set for adults. I can't wait to apply a little juice to that man as payback."

"We have to catch him first," said Ben. He had both hands to the wall too, trying to find a seam.

"We need a blow torch," said Kanti. She had already checked that Shashi wasn't at home. The Kelsos had confirmed that their son wasn't at home either. All the parents were on their way. "It has to be hollow, Alvaro. My daughter is behind that wall!"

"I'll get a torch," said Alvaro. He disappeared along the corridor.

"Men," said Kanti. She glowered at Alvaro's helpers, who were all men, daring them to say something. Feeling lightheaded, she fell into lotus position on the floor. The strength had gone from her legs. "All right, there is a brute force way of doing things and a slick way." She pointed a finger at Susan. "How did your ghost get to the other side?"

Susan shrugged. "The door opened for him. He put his forehead against the wall there and it opened."

"Maybe a nanoseal?" To those present, Juan Carlos' question was more a hopeful suggestion.

Ben went to the wall and ran his hand all around the area again, this time a little higher. Kanti stood with Susan's help and joined him, swaying from side to side from her dizziness.

"Eureka," she said when she found the grease spot where Xavier's forehead had touched the wall. "It's probably a proximity switch keyed by a subvocalized command."

"And probably to the characteristics of his voice," said Ben. "AI, do you know the key?"

"Yes," said the AI.

"Tell us what it is," said Kanti.

"I'm not at liberty to say," said the AI.

Juan Carlos had mouthed the words as the AI said them. He was becoming frustrated with the AI, although he knew very well he could do nothing about its programming—at least not right then.

"Overlay IR imaging," said Ben, changing tactics.

The ghostly outline of a door appeared in the wall. Kanti pointed to a small rectangle that surrounded the print from Xavier's forehead.

"If we hit that with ultrasound," said Ben, "it might open the door."

One of Alvaro's men was already telling Alvaro to bring along an ultrasound probe as well as the torch.

Chapter Thirty

Xavier was giving Shashi and Brian a guided tour of the secret lab. Everyone was less nervous after our little snack. I had received sweet cream instead of milk, so I was very content as I smacked my lips. Enjoy your pleasures when you can, I always say, although there were reasons to think I'd soon be euthanized.

I followed along, somewhat bored. I had talked with Shashi and Brian only a little since the AI came back on line. It was enough to impress them with my intelligence and knowledge. It was also enough to make Xavier jealous. Ergo, the tour.

As we went into the big specimen room, even I, the cynical cat, became impressed. There were all kinds of strange plants and animals, genetically modified to live underwater and to breathe in low oxygen environments, for example, at a variety of temperatures and pressures.

Xavier's explanations were brief but precise. He was adapting Earth's creatures to live off Earth in all kinds of hostile environments. At the same time, he was making some animals smarter, like me.

"I don't get it," said Brian. "If you'll pardon my asking, Mr. Paws, what use might there be for a genius cat?"

I was silent. I didn't know any answer except the obvious one that Xavier did it because he could.

"If I could experiment with humans and try to adapt them, we wouldn't need the animals right now. However, animals can do stuff we can't, and in very challenging environments. Man's future in the universe will be intimately connected to his genetic designs, including those applied to himself." He coughed with feigned modesty. "He and his animals also may need to become more intelligent. Mr. Paws was a test case on a non-Human life form. He was supposed to be euthanized shortly after I had my test data, but he provided company for me."

I had mixed emotions about Xavier's answer that partly confirmed my worse fears. I liked the part that he'd become attached to me, though. He had some positive qualities, this mad scientist!

"Sounds like you're playing God," said Brian.

"Definitely not on high moral ground," said Shashi, sensing she was going to upchuck.

"Completely justified in my case," I said.

"Yes, Mr. Paws, you'd better be on my side." Xavier pointed a gnarled finger my way. "If it weren't for me, you'd be as stupid as any other dumb house cat."

"Moreover, I wouldn't be sentient," said the AI.

"Wasn't this banned back in the 21st century?" said Shashi. "Some U.N. resolution or something?"

"Do you think I'd let some stupid rules created by stupid politicians, bureaucrats, and ethicists get in the way of my research?" said Xavier. "Obviously others think like me and support my work." He waved a hand, indicating the rows and rows of specimens. "Who do you think pays for all this?"

Brian was watching a spider monkey with finned feet and gills play at the bottom of his tank of seawater. He was building an elaborate castle out of shells but stopped long enough to make faces at the bigger primate staring in at him.

"That's a good question," he said. "Who does foot the bill?"

"I have several backers. Mr. Fabio Martínez from GenCorp is the most generous. Denise Andersen from WorldNet finances some far-out projects. They all love the progress I've made and are eager for more results."

"Why all the secrecy if it's so important?" said Shashi. She looked for a place to sit as another wave of nausea hit her. Brian let her lean against him.

"Your mother discovered what I was doing. She tried to shut me down for ethical reasons. I loved her, although I guess I valued my research more." There was some nostalgia in his voice. He stooped and picked me up. "Now, I'm afraid it's time for me to go. My friend here has been successful in bringing down my entire operation." Xavier handed me to Shashi as we all walked out of the specimen room. "Take care of him, please."

He put on a mask and, before Brian or Shashi could stop him, shot us with the spray can. I too lost consciousness.

Chapter Thirty-One

"OK. Let's try the ultrasound probe first."

Alvaro flipped a switch. He had placed the probe on the small rectangular IR outline where Xavier had put his forehead. Dialing up the power, they all waited. No one expected it to be instantaneous.

Yet the door opened. Alvaro and his men blocked it so it wouldn't close again. The others rushed inside the secret lab behind Kanti and Ben.

"Shashi!"

Kanti's scream upset many of the animals in the lab. The screeches, crows, brays, and other sounds from them reverberated from the metal walls like a deafening modern musical composition of twelve-tone cacophony.

She shook her daughter.

"Smells sickly sweet," said Susan, holding her nose.

"It's chloroform," said Kanti. "It can be used as anesthesia. Too much can produce cardiac arrhythmia. We have to move everyone to sick bay."

"Who did this?" said Alvaro, joining the other parents.

"And whose lab is this?" said Juan Carlos.

"We're not sure," said Ben, "but the name Xavier Von Weisskoph comes to mind." He looked at Kanti, who was perspiring even in the cool air of the lab.

"Never heard of him," said Susan. She directed a soundless question to Juan Carlos by raising her eyebrows. He shrugged, just as mystified as she was by the fact that the grown-ups now seemed to know what was going on.

"You will," said Ben, "but let's move your friends to sick bay. Alvaro, can you take care of things here?"

Alvaro nodded. He was already talking with Christine about what they needed to do.

***

While Alvaro, Christine, and others were trying to round up help to seal off the lab and take care of its occupants, Ruthie entered the lab through the door in the specimen room, the same door where Xavier had exited. The two men Alvaro left behind to guard the crime scene didn't get a good look at her as she shot them with a dart gun. Four trusted dockworkers followed her in, carts ready.

Timing is always of the essence, she thought. She had acted quickly when Xavier called.

"You know what to do?" They all nodded. "All this must be crated and shipped with Xavier. I want this place to be squeaky clean, to look like empty space we'd forgotten about over the years." With hands on her hips, she glared at them, making up for her size by the commanding tone of her voice. "If any of you breathes a word about this, he'll subsequently breathe vacuum. I'll say no more."

"What do we do with these two?" said the apparent leader.

"I have half a mind to throw them out of an airlock. But murder isn't one of my sins. Take them with you to the docks and leave them where they can be found."

The men grumbled a little before they started to work. Ruthie turned and left them.

We must salvage what we can. Curse the ethics!

Ruthie had already contacted GenCorp with a coded message. One of their big rigs was heading for Jupiter in a few hours. Xavier would be on it, with most of his life's work onboard—notes, computers, and live specimens.

Or he'll be dead.

Although she respected the scientist, she blamed him for letting the situation get out of hand. It was her job to put them back on course.

***

Xavier had hiding places to tide him over until the big rig launched. He was already looking forward to the trip.

I'll miss Mr. Paws. He was my one weakness. I love that damn cat!

He would now have to establish a new lab on Europa. GenCorp had its own science colony there. There wasn't any extradition to Earth and very little UNSA presence.

It would be difficult—he no longer would have the benefit of working in a micro-g environment. Jupiter's moon only had a tenth of the gravitational attraction of Earth, but the space station's spin gravity was lower.

He started to munch on a Snickers bar. *It could have been much worse. I wonder if Shashi and her friend are OK. And Mr. Paws and the AI.* He drank water out of his canteen. *A little nap can't hurt.*

He had regrets about Kanti. Years ago, he had been furious when she turned on him. But over the years, he had mellowed and valued the little time they had spent together. It had been torture for him to watch from afar as she went about her medical duties on the station. *Now far will have a very different meaning!* He shrugged. Life was full of twists and turns even he couldn't understand.

After an hour or so, Xavier noted Ruthie's four dockworkers brought numerous crates from inside the station and added them to the crates shipping out to Europa.

His cell phone rang. *Speaking of the devil!*

"You're all set. You're a lucky man. If your work weren't so damn important, I would have spaced you."

And a big hug for you too, you ugly old hag!

"My dear, if my work weren't so important, you wouldn't have such a rich retirement in your future. I suggest you take it now. Unless you want to go with me."

"I don't think I'd be able to stand all those months alone with you, you eccentric clown. You're right, maybe I will retire. But I have other problems to take care of first. *Bon voyage* and good riddance."

Xavier shut the phone and smiled. He sat, using a crate for back support, and closed his eyes.

***

When Shashi awoke, she was alone. Someone had hooked her onto monitoring equipment that was having little bubbly conversations with itself.

After some ten minutes, Kanti entered and handed Mr. Paws to her daughter. She checked both Shashi and Brian's vital signs. Shashi's vision wasn't very clear yet, and her mother knew it with the little light she shined in her daughter's eyes. It seemed that her mother was on an out-of-focus 3D imager.

"There's someone who wants to see you first, so let me fill you in. Did you know about the porn video?"

"What porn video?"

Kanti explained. "It's been resolved. Both you and Ben are off the hook. The person responsible wants to talk to you."

Kanti left. Another person entered. Shashi was surprised to see the Gnat.

"I'm terribly sorry," she said, rushing to the bed and taking Shashi's hand.

Shashi was too tired to withdraw it. *Why do I feel so weak?*

185

"You don't seem too pissed," said the Gnat.

"I've been too busy chasing this damn cat!"

"I hope you can forgive me."

Shashi was quiet for a long time, stroking the cat, who was purring.

"You must really like Brian," Shashi finally said in a whisper.

"No, stupid," said the Gnat, tears welling in her expressive eyes, "you have it all wrong! I like you! And now you think I'm dirt."

The Gnat ran out of the hospital room crying.

Shashi didn't know what to make of Natasha's outburst. Fortunately the next visitors—Kanti again, now with family and friends—took her mind away from the problem.

***

Kanti also wheeled Brian in on his gurney. "For some reason this young man wanted to see for himself that you are all right."

"Are you OK, Shashi?" said Brian. He relaxed when she nodded. "I think I received more chloroform," he said with a mumble. "Maybe closer to that spray can."

Kanti pointed to the tabby Shashi was stroking. "It's very attached to you."

"I'm not an 'it,'" said Mr. Paws, startling everyone in the room besides Shashi and Brian. "For one thing, I'm a mathematician and proud of it." He licked his front paws for a moment.

"How are you feeling, Shashi?" said Ben, still staring at the cat.

"Not well. I guess chloroform is potent stuff."

"Especially when combined with swine flu," said Kanti. "Xavier infected you and you infected me. I've ordered vaccine to be sent to us from UN-CDC. I don't know where Xavier got the virus. Obviously a number of people, especially Brian, are now exposed."

"Xavier undoubtedly received the virus in one of his many clandestine shipments," said Mr. Paws. "Xavier is resourceful. By the way, I know where he is."

Overcoming her astonishment, Kanti studied the cat.

"Now, really, how do you know that? You were out longer than Shashi and Brian."

Shashi was sitting in bed, still petting Mr. Paws. Brian was lying down, still woozy from the chloroform. Susan and Juan Carlos remained concerned; Susan sat on the edge of Shashi's gurney and Juan Carlos on Brian's.

"The trouble with this place," the cat said, "is that, as homey as it is, it isn't very big. There are many little spots to hide, especially for me. However, Xavier is big and tall like you, doc."

"And who is Xavier Von Weisskoph?" said Shashi. "Come clean, Mom."

Kanti blushed.

"It's a long story. He's actually Baron Xavier Von Weisskoph. He counts Austrian nobility in his pedigree, as if it matters nowadays."

"But he looks like Dracula," said Shashi.

"I assure you he's not a vampire," said Kanti. "He could be quite charming when he was young. But he's also very dangerous. He's a sociopath and research is his life."

"Did he give you up for his research?" said Shashi in a whisper.

"It happened before I met your father." She looked at Ben. "We all thought he'd died in a terrible fire. Ruthie sent his body back to be buried in a family plot in Vienna. We'd prefer not to talk about the details."

"You have to," said Shashi, getting out of the bed, "but not now. Mr. Paws, if you know where Xavier is, lead the way."

"I'm not a hundred per cent certain, but OK. Everyone, fall in line—Puss'n'Boots takes command!"

The cat darted out of sickbay, still swaying a little from the effects of the chloroform. Ben, Kanti, Susan, and Juan Carlos followed right behind while Shashi and Brian, still not recovered themselves, brought up the rear.

***

Xavier stepped onto the little shuttle at the last moment. After the airlock cycled, he took off his helmet. The pilot was as surprised as Xavier when a fist smashed into the scientist's face.

"You monster." Rafael was ready to deliver another blow. "How dare you put those children's lives in peril!"

Xavier wiped away the blood from his mouth and circled the astrophysicist.

"*Ach*, a young and impetuous superhero," he said. He parried Rafael's second blow and doubled him up with a blow to his midsection. "You will learn, young man, that life is not always fair."

As an example of that lesson, Rafael soon discovered he was no match for Xavier's long arms or skill at self-defense. Xavier straightened him with a left uppercut to the jaw that left his head ringing. The man in black then wrapped his arms around Rafael. They looked like they were dancing a polka until the pilot of the shuttle smashed Xavier's helmet on Rafael's head, rendering him unconscious.

"Another meddler in my affairs takes a nap," said Xavier, catching his wind while thanking the pilot with a nod. "Put his helmet on and leave him on the dock.

Hopefully someone will find him before his air runs out. If not, *c'est la meme chose*."

Xavier waited for the pilot to do his bidding.

"All the same for me too," said the pilot when he returned from his chore. "I'm sorry. I thought he was you."

Xavier smiled and spread his arms wide, looking like a scarecrow from some cornfield in Iowa. "Xavier Von Weisskph, at your service. All ahead full, Mr. Scott."

The pilot, wondering who Mr. Scott was, closed the lock and sat at the shuttle's controls. "They're still loading some stuff. Be patient. I'll have you on your way very soon."

Chapter Thirty-Two

Ruthie watched as the dockworkers stowed the last of the crates away aboard the shuttle. Xavier was already on board.

She had found Rafael on the dock and had two workers carry him to sickbay.

"Easy, easy," she had told them. "He may have a concussion."

She was so tired. She had survived crazy politicians, wacko military personnel, corporate magnates, and scientists and engineers. She had outlasted NASA, the Russians, ESA, and the Chinese. UNSA's pension was generous, and she had considerably padded it with Fabio's bonuses. With it and the savings she had squirreled away, her retirement in her favorite Downy place, Bariloche, Argentina, should be comfortable and pleasant.

It's time. I'm too old for this. Maybe I'll know if I did some good before I die.

She returned to her office, wondering what her future might bring. In particular, Bariloche seemed far away.

***

Rafael Franchetti was waiting for her, his head bandaged.

"You are efficient, Ruthie." He tossed her a memory cube. "I cannot stop your accomplice and friend. However, I think there's enough evidence here to convict you and put you away for the rest of your days. It's a little iffy on Senator Martinez and the Baron Xavier Von

Weisskoph, especially since Xavier will be on that rig. What a nice little gang."

Ruthie tossed the tiny cube up and down while looking at the face she now knew so well.

"Does Christine have one of these?"

"Why did you do it?" said Rafael. "Was Xavier's research so special?"

"I thought so. I know so." She licked her lips, feeling dehydrated. "Some people have a vision. I have had one for a long time, one of humankind reaching out for the stars. I managed to convince Fabio my vision would make him extremely wealthy. Long before Isha Bai had the same idea." The memory module seemed heavy. *You're adding the weight of your years, woman.* "I always thought that, independent of Fabio's support, we needed to continue our evolution. We need to adapt to different environments if we are to survive out here." She sat, exhaustion winning over defiance. "You were out doing your spacewalk and overcame your fear. However, your phobia must have hammered home the fact that space is not our natural environment. To go to the stars we need to adapt."

"Quite a speech. What were you, Martinez' mistress? Hard to believe a prim young general from Singapore could give that toad the time of day."

"Fabio as a young man had his moments—wealthy, witty, dashing, and a great entertainer. You're right, though; he's motivated by greed and power, especially as he grows older. I used him. I have this knack for using people. I'm a control freak."

"You can't control everything, clearly. A young girl's love for a cat, for example. Or, the curiosity of her and her friends. You crashed the AI, didn't you?"

Ruthie shrugged. "It doesn't matter. Xavier escaped and will continue his research on Europa. Fabio will continue to finance that research."

"And they will continue to play God. Maybe Dr. Bai can do something about that; maybe she can't. Your retirement will be spent in the moon's penal colony."

"I don't think so. I'll repeat my question: have you given a copy of the data cube to Christine?"

"Not yet."

"Good. I recommend you seriously think about destroying the original and all copies."

"Why would I do that?"

"Because you're my son."

Rafael Franchetti stared at her, his lips quivering. "I-I don't believe you! How can that be?" He tried to sit and almost fell off the low chair.

"You were adopted, weren't you? We can do a DNA test if you want, although I'm ninety-nine point ninety-nine per cent certain you are the baby I gave up for adoption during my sojourn in Argentina when I was the military attaché for Singapore. I believed in genetics engineering even back then. They had a long history of supporting such research from the time the Nazis sought asylum there." She winked at him. "I'd say you turned out very well. Just call me Mama." Her smile was wide—and surprisingly tender.

***

"He was here," said Mr. Paws, dropping the candy wrapper at Kanti's feet. "There are a couple of other places." He listed them as the AI plotted them in a holographic map. "We should split up."

Shashi, Brian, and Mr. Paws went to the first location, Ben and Susan to the second, and Kanti and Juan Carlos to the third. The first location was near the shuttle docks.

"I guess he's not a bad person," said Shashi on the way there. She was leaning on Brian for support now.

"I guess," said Brian. "But he could have killed us."

"Hey, he gave me life," said Mr. Paws. "I had my problems with him, but I think he's lost his way. You Humans seem to do that a lot."

"Philosophy from a cat," said Brian.

"Not just any cat," said Shashi. "Look, isn't that a big rig off in the distance?"

The structure's metal beams caught the intense sunlight. The rig was visible, although they had moored it in LEO a good distance away from the space station.

"AI, can you identify that ship?"

"It's the *Aguila*. It will carry supplies to the various colonies and scientific stations on Europa."

"When is it leaving?" said Mr. Paws.

"In four minutes," said the AI.

They knew the ship was four to five football fields long, a planar array of girders. Its cargo was strapped down along the girders. They also knew that somewhere on that ship Xavier was hiding.

The ship's nuclear engines fired and two new stars joined the ones in the firmament. The nanos in the port in the airlock's door darkened in response to the intense light.

Shashi watched the big rig crawl out of LEO on its way to the outer planets. She suspected they would soon discover Xavier onboard. She picked up Mr. Paws and stroked him.

"What will they do with Xavier?" she said.

Brian gave her a hug.

"He'll be all right. It's what he wants. He and your mother were too close."

"I know. It's sad."

"He's a strange Human," said Mr. Paws, as Brian joined in the petting. "I'm fond of him. It's just me and the AI now."

"And us," said Shashi.

"Can we stay together?" said Mr. Paws.

"I don't know," said Brian. "After all the trouble you've caused?"

Mr. Paws bit his hand, but it was a love nip because the cat was purring.

"We can still use some secret help with our calculus homework from time to time," said Shashi.

"I can do that in my sleep." The cat kneaded Shashi's shoulder with his claws. "Right now I can use some fresh milk. Anyone game for refreshments?"

***

On the *Aguila* Xavier stretched out on his bunk. He was watching a classic sci-fi movie called *Star Wars: The Last Jedi* and sipping from a glass of ten-year-old shiraz wine.

His stateroom was comfortable. Senator Martinez knew how to take care of honored guests. He figured he deserved the R & R he would have over the next few months.

His free hand reached to pet Mr. Paws. He frowned as it stopped in midair.

Luxury is overrated, he told himself, as he dabbed at the cut at the corner of his mouth again.

Epilogue

So there you have it.

The AI and I became famous for a while until the news media found something else to report. Without the plants and animals in the secret lab as evidence, he and I became a simple curiosity for visiting scientists. People had problems believing our story.

In particular, UNSA Security could not pin anything on Senator Martinez. And, to this day, no one has been able to get past the blocks Xavier put on the AI's memory.

I always suspected Rafael Franchetti knew a lot more than he was telling. No one knew where he had been those final hours. When Ruth Ellen MacGregor retired, it was curious Rafael and the Kelsos were there at the shuttle to see her off. I had no idea they were close.

Alvaro became the new station administrator. He and Rafael had become close friends, and stayed friends, even when Rafael received a post on one of Saturn's moons.

Alvaro's son, Juan Carlos, won an internship on Earth's moon and eventually became physical plant administrator for the Farside complex. He recovered from his hang-up about trying to be a Latin lover and married a lovely astrophysicist there who was studying neutrino showers. I haven't heard from him lately. I know he's in contact with the rest of the Fearsome Four. They all remain good friends.

The Gnat lost her nickname. She publicly admitted to starting all the gossip and said she was very sorry. She took an internship with Christine Bauer and quickly learned the ins and outs of station security. She and

Susan are now in a romantic relationship and writing all kinds of code for the next generation of organic computers. More surprisingly, Natasha and Shashi finally became good friends.

My, how Humans can change!

Ben and Kanti eventually mated—tied the knot, got hitched—whatever Humans call it. They are busy making kittens—smelly little Humans that are the most helpless creatures. I was jealous at first because Kanti had adopted me, so to speak. She still gave me enough attention that I only occasionally yearned for a petting from Shashi or one of the Fearsome Four.

Shashi and Brian also married, though much later. Their future is far from LEO as they went to join Rafael's team on that Saturn moon to do some of their own research on atmospheres of gas giant planets.

I wrote this all up and published it an Earth zine specializing in conspiracy theories. Ruth Ellen tried to block it. She wouldn't say why. I ignored her, but I had to publish it as fiction, trying to fill in the gaps relating to her. The controversy melted away with her retirement.

Writing this story was very difficult. My math papers and textbooks are a lot easier, believe me. Sometimes I'm called Professor Paws now, although my only teaching responsibility in the past was to help the Fearsome Four. They had a lot of difficulty with differential equations after calculus.

You may wonder why I'm still alive. Some of Kanti's research on telomeric extension has led to a much increased lifespan. She doesn't know if it's a good thing considering the billions of Downy wretches living below. I have no doubts. I suppose someday I'll have to join my ancestors. Right now, I'm having too much fun.

I'm such a celebrity that I'm often one of the honored invitees at state dinners in the Sky Lounge. I have even given a speech or two. I don't go often, though. Humans, especially politicians, can be very boring sometimes, unless they're causing all sorts of problems....

Note from A. B. Carolan

Thank you for reading this new edition of *The Secret Lab*. Mr. Paws also thanks you. Please write a review on Amazon, Facebook, Goodreads, Smashwords, your blog—wherever you find other readers interested in books—so they and I know what you like and dislike about it. Especially do so if you're a young adult or the parent of one—I'd like your feedback.

Coming soon in the ABC Sci-Fi Mysteries for Young Adults: *The Secret of the Urns*. Watch for it! A preview follows...

The following is a preview of A. B. Carolan's The Secret of the Urns...

Chapter One

My leg was broken. *Way to go, girl!*

That wasn't my only worry. Kids break bones all the time. Hard Fist's climate would kill me, not the break.

There wasn't likely to be anyone near, and no one knew where I was. I didn't even know, and, even if I did, I couldn't communicate the location to anyone. Nobody within yelling distance, and even radio signals would be blocked where I lay flat on my back in pain.

Although it was still hot, the white sun had just gone down behind the precipice's edge, leaving me in shadow, except for Big Fellow's pale light dominating the twilight sky of its satellite Hard Fist. Soon night would fall, temperatures would plummet, and I would freeze.

At least the ubiquitous sounds from the satellite's rainforest had started up again to provide me with some funeral music. Of course, those sounds would make the dirge a bit primitive; some might even say they were threatening. You could almost hear chanted words to the effect, "Humans don't belong here!" *Yeah, tell my parents that!*

My usual cheery thirteen-year-old innocence and positive outlook on life had suffered a major blow along with my leg. I was thinking they'd morphed into stupidity instead. Fact is, I'm not stupid—I'm the child of a triad that had bioengineered my mental and physical attributes as well as they could, given the genetic material they had available, which was AOK considering each member of the triad had the same thing done for them. But I'd just acted stupidly, so I could almost hear old Darwin crowing about natural selection being the better choice.

So far, growing up on Hard Fist hadn't been easy. The planet-sized moon orbits the gas giant Big Fellow, almost a star itself and about twice the size of Jupiter. This largest planet in the Fistian star system lies at the E-zone's edge, so its satellite is theoretically habitable, but barely so in practice, at least for Humans. Some of my difficulties growing up there had their origin in the harsh environment. *And now it might kill me!*

Hard Fist broke all the rules. Tides were huge due to Big Fellow's proximity. When they combined with strong winds from a storm, lowlands close to the shore flooded, so communities weren't found close to the shore. Lush tropical forests took advantage of 0.9 relative to E-normal gravity and the greenhouse effect, but all that vegetation also saturated the air with free oxygen while fixing excess nitrogen. The whole atmosphere is in a strange equilibrium that scientists were just beginning to understand. Other nearby but smaller satellites toyed with Big Fellow's powerful attraction enough to keep our moon from being tide-locked to the gas giant, another precarious equilibrium, although that didn't matter much because Big Fellow wasn't a star. These were strange equilibriums that had lasted for eons, though. I'd never wanted to understand their intricacies, but we all suffered from their capricious nature.

Even in the 21st century, Human scientists knew there were many planets in near-Earth space. Turned out many are habitable; in other words, there are many places where Humans can live. At the personal level, though, people don't have to like living in those places. For my tenure on Hard Fist, I had no choice. I couldn't leave my legal wardens, my parents, until I was eighteen—or, unless I received their permission to do so, which I'd been on the verge of asking many times recently. Because I was often invisible to them in a manner of speaking, having a chance to ask or receive permission wasn't likely to happen anytime soon, though. I did the best I could to cope.

I had difficulties with grown-ups in general. Most of these problems could be traced to their not remembering what it was like to be a kid. They were mostly scientists, engineers, and other technical people who were sent to Hard Fist to study that strange moon. While there should have been a law against it, some of them had kids. I'm one of those. My name is Asako Kobayashi, a Human Fistian, the first one. Others followed, but I'm unique, as if that mattered. *Write that on my funeral urn, Mom and Dad2.* Of course, they might never find my body!

***

Humans had found native Fistians on Hard Fist—we didn't know how many exactly, but certainly a lot more than Humans. The Human grown-ups didn't socialize with them. The "official reason" was that they were studying native Fistians and everything else Fistian, the entire biosphere, in other words, so they didn't want to lose their objectivity.

By the time I turned ten (Earth standard years, not Fistian years), I knew the real reason: Humans generally didn't like native Fistians. Some even expressed their prejudices openly, especially recent arrivals. Others never admitted to having them but exhibited them through their actions. Almost everyone considered the moon's natives barely sentient and primitive. I knew better.

My parents were a lot more understanding than some. They allowed me to play with Marcello, my Fistian friend.

I needed that playtime because all the other Human kids were much younger, many just babies. I knew most of Marcello's clan too. I named the clan mother, the cultural and political boss, Mama Dora. She's about as ancient and tough as anyone could seem to be for a young girl of thirteen. You don't fool around with Mama Dora.

Marcello, my best friend, is way down in the pecking order in his village and about four or five generations removed from Mama Dora as near as I could tell. Three times my size—still small compared to a grown male—he is gentle and has a great sense of humor. He'd play tricks on me, like the time he jumped out in front of me on the road coming home from school one day and made me scream.

The Fistian young don't go to our school. That never made sense to me either. They pick up languages faster than Humans, for example. While I struggled with the dead but "classic" languages English and Mandarin—ones we only see in computer history files or hear in ancient videos—Marcello spoke them fluently, as well as Standard, that mish-mash of the two languages, with lots of bits and pieces from others, that had developed among Spacers back in the home solar system.

I once saw a drawing of a centaur in a video called "Mythical Creatures of Earth"—yeah, it was in old English. Other Humans on Hard Fist used the word in a derogatory sense, so I'd become curious and queried Einstein, the camp's AI, about it. Marcello looks a little bit like a centaur. He's harder to ride because his back slopes at a thirty degree angle from his butt up to his head—not like a horse's body at all (a few non-mythological Earth creatures had survived the Tali invasion of Earth and were taken to other near-Earth systems, so I'd seen videos of live horses).

You have to sprawl on top of Marcello and hold on to his thick mane for dear life as he gallops through the forest, pawing branches aside with those big hands and strong arms, laughing via snorts and grinning with his dancing eyebrows while I scream for him to slow down. In fact, one time he suddenly did, just to piss me off. I went sailing into a scummy pond. He stood on the bank, swishing at swamp flies with his thick tail, and bellowed out his laughter. A real comedian.

It took me a week to get the stench out of my hair. It took me two to forgive him.

***

The day I broke my leg I hadn't been able to find Marcello. A member of his clan told me he'd gone hunting in the high country. I liked the high country—it was a little cooler there in the daytime, which was nice, and much colder at night, which wasn't. I was upset that he hadn't taken me with him, so I went to find him. *Big mistake!*

There are no volcanoes on Hard Fist, but there are rivers of lava. The huge gravitational pull from Big Fellow kneads the satellite, about the size of Earth, into a wrinkled elastic ball with many cracks all over it. The thermal activity created at its core, so visible from space, more than compensates for being on the E-zone's cold edge. Add the greenhouse effect, and you have a tropical climate, except at the poles, but one with wide temperature swings between day and night.

The lava rivers don't flow like rivers, though, because the cracks in the mantle begin, wander a bit in a north-south direction, and then end. The Fistians work around them. Those rivers are especially beautiful when one terminus reaches out into the ocean, and the crack becomes an angry fjord complete with a crashing kilometers-wide waterfall where seawater turns into steam. That water vapor rises, condenses into clouds, and rains down on the lush forests filled with flora and fauna so varied that our scientists haven't even begun to catalog all the species.

Enter the drooler, the most feared predator prowling under the rainforest's tall canopy. Preying on everything from the large insect-like four-winged creatures to its own kind, alive or carrion, this fellow is a lumbering eating machine. I hadn't counted on meeting one, though. They were solitary beasts and only sociable when you look like food.

We call them droolers because they slobber as they walk. Behind all the slobbers, they have plenty of sharp teeth—that doesn't add anything to their charm. They are nasty, vile creatures that will even take on an adult Fistian to get a full meal, but they'll also eat Humans as appetizers.

Most of the time, though, droolers are slow enough that you can run away from them. That's easy to do because they smell like algae rotting in a 'ponics tank. We Humans don't have a keen sense of smell, but we can still smell a drooler about two or three klicks away. A native Fistian can pick up that odor from an even greater distance. In either case, the strategy is clear: you just make sure you move away from the drooler's stench. Other directions aren't recommended.

I figured local fauna should be able to detect a drooler's stench as well as or better than a native Fistian, so I wondered how the stinky creatures caught anything to eat. There were conjectures about them hunting in packs so their prey wouldn't have anywhere to go as the circle around them closed. Hard to say whether the conjecture had any substance because no Human had seen packs of droolers. On the contrary, they seemed like solitary beasts, so maybe fresh meat was caught by accident, and they mostly dined on carrion.

I wasn't about to go looking for droolers to find out more about them. But this one had found me.

He was a youngster, though, and moved about as fast as I did. (I say "he" because the males have bright blue-green balls that are conspicuous even at a distance—the rest of the tan body is dappled with light and dark green spots.) Junior was also persistent.

The ubiquitous blister vines whipped across my face and body as I fled through the forest, receiving a bloody gash above my eye and on my left breast. Their oily residue stung like hell, and the pain slowed me down. Think of semi-sentient and slightly mobile poison ivy on steroids, live whips that liked to pommel and grab.

Did I mention they sing? Little suckers along their lengths breathe in and out, making a high-pitched humming noise. (Unlike centaurs, poison ivy isn't mythical Earth flora, but it's long gone from planet Earth, thanks to the Tali invasion.) Their whipping action makes a bit of noise too.

The young drooler was just about to sink his teeth into me when I broke out into the clear and flew over the edge of the precipice, right across one of those lava rifts. This one was narrow enough that I didn't fall in and become deep-fried Asako tempura, a fate I thought might still be better than being eaten by this carnivore. I hit a ledge four meters down on the opposite side so hard that I broke my leg and knocked the wind out. My pursuer, moving a bit slower, hit only the edge of the ledge, clawed desperately for a few seconds, and then crashed into the molten lava many meters below.

I felt sorry for him. He wouldn't be able to breed and pass his stupidity on to his offspring.

I then realized that the same could be said of me.

Author Note

You have just finished the sci-fi mystery *The Secret Lab*. We know you have many reading choices these days, so we're honored you've chosen to read this book.

Here's a bonus for avid readers: we can't publish everything we write—even the good stuff (the bad stuff never sees the light of day, of course)—so you can find free stuff at Steve's website http://stevenmmoore.com . Free short stories can be found in his blog category "ABC Shorts" or "Steve's Shorts," and PDFs free for the asking are listed on the "Free Stuff & Contests" webpage. For the latter, just query Steve using the contact page at his website, or email me at steve@stevenmmoore.com.

See Steve's entire list of novels at his website http://stevenmmoore.com or at his Amazon author page.

For news about reading, writing, and publishing, see Steve's online newsletter "News and Notices from the Writing Trenches"; you can also sign up for his email newsletter by writing him at steve@stevenmmoore.com. The two newsletters are complementary...and complimentary.

In libris libertas...

Notes, References, and Disclaimers

You might have figured out that this is the second edition of the young adult sci-fi mystery *The Secret Lab*; Steven M. Moore wrote the first edition, and he kindly let me rewrite and reedit it for this new print edition. Everything else is new too, including the cover, and the novel takes its rightful place in the ABC sci-fi mysteries for young adults. Isaac Asimov wrote the first sci-fi mysteries, but this one is for young adults and adults who are young-at-heart.

For the science, main plot, and the intertwining themes of the story, I couldn't improve much on Steve's book. So, read on, to find the "Notes, References, and Disclaimers" from that first edition (my comments are found in square brackets).

As usual, this novel wouldn't be in your hands without the help of kind people who helped put it together: Donna Carrick, an important author in her own right and able director of Carrick Publishing, did the formatting for this print edition. Sara Carrick did a masterful job on the new cover. Of course, Steve wants to thank all those who reviewed or commented on the first edition—I took them into consideration for this second edition.

Finally, my thanks go to Steve and his lovely wife, whose love for cats permeates this story. They tell me they've known cats who seem almost as intelligent as Mr. Paws. By the way, Steve isn't dead…he's just too busy writing other stories, so I'm helping out. The next book in this YA series, *The Secret of the Urns*, will be all mine (Bela Lugosi-style chortle with wringing of the hands).

A. B. Carolan
Donegal, Ireland
January 2018

A.B. CAROLAN

Extracts from the first edition:

This novel takes place in a far future when the International Space Station has morphed into a major transportation hub for the exploration and exploitation of our home star system. I have postulated a chaotic growth (with the demise of the U.S. shuttle program, we can wonder if there will be much, if at all). You will find none of the orderly pinwheels of Clarke and Kubrick's *2001* or the space operas of our childhoods. Imagine the uncontrolled growth of a mining town in California during the Gold Rush, although this space town grows in 3D, with all the antennas, power modules, solar panels, etc, needed for a viable space community.

I have strived hard to make this novel more than Harry Potter in outer space. I recognize there is a fuzzy boundary between fantasy and sci-fi, yet I believe there is enough magic in the logical extrapolation of present day science and technology that we don't need wizards, witches, and warlocks. Or vampires and werewolves, for that matter....

It is difficult to extrapolate computer technology. Sentience in computers is treated in *2001* with HAL becoming somewhat of a disembodied villain for the astronauts on their way to Jupiter (Clarke and Kubrick thereby succumbing to the Frankenstein complex). Heinlein wrote a more favorable treatment where the computer in *The Moon is a Harsh Mistress* becomes one of the heroes in a lunar revolt. The AI (Artificial Intelligence) in *The Secret Lab* is more ambiguous. It tries to agree with both camps and finds itself in trouble while trying to please everyone.

Computer hardware is another issue. We have progressed from huge mainframe installations with false floors and air conditioning to huge server farms…with false floors and air conditioning; from mainframe terminals as dummy extensions to the mainframe, to the desktop computer, and finally to powerful laptops and desktops networked to all those servers (cloud computing is just networked computing). I can only extrapolate what I know. Long ago, though, I came up with the idea that desktop devices would become just engines to power games and visualization software and that much of the machine-to-human interconnectivity would be realized with extensions of the cochlear implant and voice recognition technology. Tomorrow's advances might date all my material —hopefully, the story that remains is still entertaining.

As we know from Dolly, the sheep, and the introduction of the new and improved form of Atlantic salmon, gene manipulation is real, not science fiction. [I agree with avoiding the pejorative acronym GMO, because all current dogs, cats, and tulips are genetically modified creations.] Of course, we may be a long way from making a Mr. Paws or an Orson. The 21st century will probably be known as the century of engineering genetics. How do we balance arguments for improved food production and new, targeted cancer drugs with ideas like cloning? The associated ethical questions that arise will be fiercely debated—I have already read and heard many emotional rants on the subject. I hope the debate will take a less emotional turn in the future. By introducing the subject to young readers as I do in this novel, I will have perhaps encouraged a saner debate among the next generations.

Mr. Paws refers to the Kzins. Larry Niven created them ("The Warriors," a short story in the original Man-Kzin Wars collection, 1966). Writing Known Space stories has become a major industry for other sci-fi writers (twelve volumes strong at my last count, plus various offshoot story collections). I personally don't think the theme of connecting predatory behavior with intelligence is treated well enough in any of these stories (human beings are undoubtedly the most fearsome predators on our planet). However, it's natural that Mr. Paws has read them and has opinions on the subject.

The idea of research hidden from public scrutiny due to its strategic or possibly unethical nature is not new in fiction or in fact. The idea of hiding it on a cramped space station is original as far as I know. I used Xavier's near invisibility to give a tip of the hat to H. G. Wells and his *The Invisible Man*. Wells was the first English language sci-fi author in my opinion, a pioneer in the genre.

The name Helldog plays homage to Mike Mignola's comic book character Hellboy and Lord Thavas to Edgar Rice Burroughs' evil scientist Ras Thavas. If Wells was the pioneer, Burroughs was the commercial sci-fi master bar none—many of his names, especially from the Martian stories, populate the Star Wars movies. Although the latter are more fantasy than sci-fi [George Lucas has admitted as much], a role-playing fantasy game for the actors [in the movie], the former led to a revolution in Hollywood special effects and its influence propagates to *Blade Runner* (and other Phillip K. Dick "classics"), *Alien*, and other more serious film entries into the sci-fi genre.

The plight of the cheetahs and Sumatran tigers is very real.

About the Authors

Steven M. Moore wrote the first edition of *The Secret Lab*. Born in California, Steve reversed the adage "Go West, young man," living twelve years in South America before settling in the Northeast. His training as a mathematician and physicist and his interests in robotics, genetics, and scientific ethics are evident in his storytelling. Although he writes mysteries, thrillers, and sci-fi, it is the human condition that intrigues him—those idiosyncrasies and crazy internal contradictions that plague us all. He also believes that humanity's only salvation is for society to encourage creative individuals who "think outside the box."

The story of the Fearsome Four and Mr. Paws was a light-hearted detour from such serious matters—it is serious fun, though, as some of the themes treated in *The Secret Lab* are very important ones.

Steve is now a full-time writer. After many years in the Boston area, his wife and he now make their home in New Jersey.

Visit him at his website http://stevenmmoore.com where you will find excerpts and other freebies as well as a blog that contains many posts that comment on current events and the writing business, book and movie reviews, and interviews. You can also find Steve on Facebook, where he counts Carrick Publishing's Donna and Alex Carrick among his many Facebook friends.

A. B. Carolan wrote this second edition of *The Secret Lab*. It's rumored that he's a descendant of the great Irish harpist and songwriter Turlough O'Carolan. Whether true or not, people also say he was a child who was stolen and raised by leprechauns. He now lives in Donegal, Ireland, where he communicates frequently with his friend Steven M. Moore.

THE SECRET LAB

A.B. CAROLAN

www.ingramcontent.com/pod-product-compliance
Lightning Source LLC
Chambersburg PA
CBHW031307120626
46554CB00001BA/320